THE HOUSE OF CARE

A NOVEL

by

W. J. BURLEY

WALKER AND COMPANY
NEW YORK

BY THE SAME AUTHOR:

DEATH IN WILLOW PATTERN
TO KILL A CAT
GUILT EDGED
DEATH IN A SALUBRIOUS PLACE
DEATH IN STANLEY STREET
WYCLIFFE AND THE PEA GREEN BOAT
WYCLIFFE AND THE SCHOOLGIRLS
THE SCHOOLMASTER
CHARLES AND ELIZABETH

Copyright © 1981 by W. J. Burley

First published in the United States of America in 1982 by
the Walker Publishing Company, Inc.

ISBN: 0-8027-5464-3

Library of Congress Catalog Card Number: 81-71201

Printed in the United States of America

10 9 8 7 6 5 4 3 2 1

Chapter One

THE THREE WOMEN sat around the table in the great bare kitchen with its tall cupboards, its stone sink and Aga range. The discoloured face of the wall-clock showed ten minutes to nine and the brass pendulum seemed to oscillate frenetically behind its little window. The three women sat and stared at the remnants of a coffee and toast breakfast.

Abruptly, Celia got up, pushed back her chair so that the legs screeched over the stone floor, and said, 'I'll make some more coffee.'

She said this every morning at the same time. Celia was thirty-eight, slim, with straight black hair, a long neck and a small head which suggested some sort of bird—a notion strengthened by her quick, darting movements which seemed to be both nervous and aggressive. She was Henry's first cousin. Eighteen years before, pregnant and with no marriage prospect, she had come to live at Nanselow as a temporary expedient and she had been there ever since so that her daughter, Alice, knew no other home.

Nancy Care, a year or two younger than Celia, was another brunette, shapely and more relaxed. She was Sir Henry's second wife and they had a son, John, who was fifteen and had been brought up with Alice as brother and sister.

Nancy began collecting the dirty dishes, piling them together.

The third woman was Isobel, Henry's sister; almost fifty, plump, and a spinster. Isobel had a mass of sandy brown hair, girlish features and freckles. She wrote romantic novels with only moderate success, smoked filter-tipped cigarettes from which she dropped ash into her saucer, and contributed to a couple of magazines for teenaged girls.

Over the years the three women had evolved a routine which, by its ritual character, allowed them to live together, if not in harmony then without frequent or serious quarrels. Later, Nancy would go off to her nursery-garden—an integral part of NEMP—Nancy's Economic Miracle Programme, designed to prop up the shaky economy of the estate; Celia would begin her household chores, and Isobel would withdraw to the library to resume work at her typewriter.

Celia, with her housekeeping, thought that she worked harder than the others and sought consolation in a low-key grumbling of which nobody took any notice. Her present grievance concerned Harold, one of Sir Henry's twin children by his first wife, now twenty-two. Harold had arrived home the previous evening having been sacked from his job with a firm of London wine importers in which his great-uncle was a partner.

'One more to get meals for, and I can't see him cleaning his room, changing his bed, or doing his own washing. If I don't do it his room will stink in a week or two.'

Isobel crushed out a cigarette and threw the butt in the general direction of the fuel bucket. 'It can't be worse than Laura's with those damned joss-sticks of hers. Just shut the door and let it stink.'

Celia gave her an angry look but made no direct reply. 'How long is he going to be home?' The question was addressed to Nancy, Lady Care.

'How should I know? Until he gets another job, I suppose.'

Celia poured boiling water into the percolator. 'One of them is bad enough but with the pair of them in the house . . . I can feel the tension rising already; it will be just like it used to be in their school vacs.'

Isobel said, 'You did more than your share of spoiling them when they were young.'

Celia slammed down the coffee pot. 'Yes, well, those who do nothing can't be blamed for making mistakes, can they?'

Isobel, observing the rules of brinkmanship, let the challenge pass. 'They're neurotic, like their mother.' This was a flag of truce.

Henry's first wife, Deborah, was a tacitly agreed scapegoat; she had died sixteen years before when the twins were six.

Whenever the three women were together for more than a few minutes the most innocent sounding topic could become controversial; words were charged with significance beyond their context; obscure allusions, meaningless to a stranger, could raise the emotional temperature to flashpoint but the three had developed the techniques of brinkmanship to a fine art and explosions were rare.

An almost imperceptible movement of the air and they were joined by Laura, Harold's twin. She was flaxen haired, fragile and delicate as a Meissen figure, with a peaches-and-cream complexion and lips which, though natural, looked as though they had been applied with the finest brush. But she wore gold-rimmed spectacles with large circular lenses which magnified her blue eyes and gave her a compelling stare. She moved with an effortless smoothness apparently unrelated to bones, joints and muscles and the mechanics of the human form. She wore a loose, plain-brown linen dress, and suspended from a thin chain round her neck, a bronze figure of a centaur bending his bow—her birth sign—Sagittarius.

'Is that the time?' Laura glanced up at the clock. She reached down a cup and saucer from one of the tall cupboards, Nancy passed her the coffee pot and she poured herself some black coffee.

Nancy said, 'No milk, today?'

'No, I'll take it black.'

She finished her coffee, picked up the string and bead affair which served as a handbag, and left by the back door. A moment or two later they heard the whine of her Mini reversing over the cobbles.

Laura and another girl had a shop in Truro which sold everything for the aspiring occultist, from incense sticks to tarot cards, from amulets and talismans to horoscopes and books on esoteric cults of great variety. There were framed texts from the works of Aleister Crowley, reproductions of engravings from Eliphas Levi and a selection of hardware for ritual magic of all kinds.

Isobel lit another cigarette. 'Slimming again. If she isn't careful she will snap in the middle.'

Nancy poured herself a fresh cup of coffee. 'There's something wrong with Laura. I'm sure it must be something psychological; could it be anorexia?'

Celia snorted with a near approach to laughter. 'At twenty-two? Don't be daft, Nancy! If little Miss Muffet hasn't come to terms with her sex by now she'll find her menopause catching up on her puberty.'

Nancy's voice hardened. 'I was only saying that I think there's something wrong with her and that she probably needs help.'

'Then you're the best one to help her; I believe in leaving ill alone in that quarter.'

The kitchen clock struck nine on its tinny gong and Isobel glanced at her watch. 'What's happened to our lord and master this morning?'

Within a minute or two Sir Henry arrived. He came into the kitchen wearing a waterproof tunic and trousers covered with paint stains and a straw hat. He carried a haversack slung over his shoulder and an easel and canvas under his arm. Sir Henry Care was forty-eight, of slight build, with reddish-gold hair that was turning grey and a thin wisp of beard that made him look like a Chinese mandarin. His eyes were dark blue and disarming in their innocence.

He looked from one to the other of the women, vaguely apprehensive, 'Has Miss Pearl been over with the post yet?'

'Not yet, dear.'

Miss Pearl worked with Captain Holiday, Henry's agent and general factotum, in the estate office behind the stable block and all the post was delivered there.

Nancy passed him the coffee she had poured for herself. 'Here, drink this, dear, it's freshly made.'

'Thank you, Nancy, I can just do with that.' He put his gear on the floor and sat down at the table but changed his mind and stood up again. 'I shall paint from the punt this morning; I think the tide and the light will be just right, and with no wind to speak of I shall

8

get reflections in the water.' He gestured uncertainly and his voice died away. The women made no response.

Henry Care was a clever gardener and an indifferent painter; perversely he thought little of his gardening skills but secretly believed that one day he would be recognized as a painter of note. The fact that one of his pictures had been nodded through for a Summer Exhibition at Burlington House had been more than enough encouragement. He held provincial exhibitions and even sold some pictures but he made no money to speak of.

He finished his coffee and picked up his load. 'I haven't been in to see mother this morning, perhaps you will tell her—'

'That you want to catch the light. Yes, dear, I'll tell her when I take up her tray directly.'

As Henry closed the door behind him it was as though the three women resumed their normal personalities after an interval wearing masks.

Isobel said, 'I think we have a Monet phase coming on.'

Nancy got up from the table, 'I'll get Ethel's tray.'

Ethel Care, Henry's mother, was seventy-seven. Alert, vigorous and resolute, she made a single concession to age—breakfast in bed.

Celia started to wash the dishes in a plastic bowl placed in the stone sink. She swept back a straying lock of hair with a damp arm. 'Some day somebody will have to start saying what they mean in this house.'

Isobel pushed back her chair and stood up. 'God help us when that happens! Remind me to be out that day. Anyway, I've got work to do; perhaps you will ask Miss Pearl to drop my mail in the library.'

Celia looked after her as she closed the door. '*She*'s got work to do!' Celia rinsed the milk jug and set it down with a bang. 'I can't take much more of the way things are going, Nancy. I know it's a family matter and nothing to do with me but ten years ago the National Trust would have taken over the estate and allowed us to continue living here; now I doubt if they'd look at it. What's going to happen to us? We're none of us getting any younger and what have we got to look forward to?'

9

Nancy tried to be soothing; she had too many misgivings of her own to encourage Celia's. 'It may not turn out as bad as you think; things could work out. If Lucille leaves her money to the twins as she promised, Harold could carry on.'

Lucille was the twins' maternal aunt, widow of a wealthy Parisian businessman.

Celia spluttered with exasperation. 'You're as bad as Henry, Nancy! How old is Lucille? Forty-five? Forty-six? She could marry again tomorrow and even if she doesn't it could be thirty or forty years before the twins see a penny of her money. For God's sake try to be realistic. If something isn't done with this place in the next four or five years it will be too late. In any case, if the twins got Lucille's money do you think they'd spend it on the estate? Not Laura, that's for sure, and as for Harold . . .'

Nancy said, 'I sometimes think we underestimate Harold; he's got more feeling for the place than we give him credit for.'

Celia was contemptuous. 'Feeling is one thing; guts is another. Harold is gutless.'

Nancy sometimes wondered where Celia kept her Christian forbearance; she was a practising Catholic; Mass on Sundays and holy days, confession as prescribed. Isobel dismissed Celia's religion as superstition—'Three Hail Marys and an Our Father to ward off the evil eye'—but Nancy allowed her the benefit of the doubt.

'All right, Celia. What would you do?'

Celia gave herself a little time to think, emptying the washing-up bowl and flushing the sink. 'I'd sell one of the farms and use the money to put the house and the estate in better order, but you'll never persuade Henry to get rid of any of his precious land until he loses the lot.'

'There isn't one of our tenants who could afford to buy '

'They could raise a mortgage like anybody else.'

'At present interest rates? They've got a job to make ends meet as it is.'

Celia shrugged. 'That's what you say; that's what Henry says, but nobody tries it on. We just sit back and wait like . . . like people on a rock waiting for the tide to come in and cut them off.'

Nancy prepared her mother-in-law's tray; a pot of tea, two thin slices of bread-and-butter, a jug of milk and a bowl for the cat . . . When it was ready she carried it upstairs to the first floor, to the bedroom over the front door. Everywhere worn carpets, faded wallpapers, damp patches and crumbling plaster told their own tale. Nancy sighed.

'Good morning, mamma.'

'Good morning, Nancy.'

Ethel was big boned with strong features; her hair had retained more than a memory of its original gold and her voice had kept its resonance. She was a Care by birth as well as marriage for she had married her first cousin. She was sitting up in bed, stroking her marmalade cat.

'I haven't seen John or Alice this morning, they usually look in on their way to school.'

'It's half-term, mamma; they've gone off in the dinghy; they were away before seven o'clock.'

The old lady nodded. 'I must be losing my wits; I'd forgotten that they're off school this week. I hope you told them not to go below Turnaware?'

'No, mamma, I didn't. You know as well as I do that it wouldn't have been any use.'

Ethel chuckled. 'You're right there! But I've nearly drowned more than once in Carrick Roads. The wind springs up from nowhere and the tides . . . We used to have an old tub of a boat with a brown lug-sail and we'd go right out between the castles and into the bay. No life-jackets then! People now-a-days expect to fall in.'

Nancy was looking out of the window. Although the view from her own room and from all the rooms in the front of the house was the same she never tired of it. Nanselow stood at the head of the shallow valley which sloped to a creek of the Fal and from the house one could see the broad shining estuary with a distant prospect of Pendennis Head, the castle like a slim cut-out against the sky.

11

She thought, I should miss it. How I should miss it! And Celia's words acquired a greater poignancy, 'Like people on a rock, waiting for the tide to come in and cut them off.'

The old lady continued to reminisce. 'That must have been early in the first war. I remember one summer when we had a French girl staying with us; she was a daughter of one of the Bordeaux wine families with whom grandfather did business. Hycinthe, she was called—a straight-laced little prude with her rosary and her missal. "*Il n'y a pas de quoi rire, Eth-el!*"' Ethel laughed so much she disturbed the cat who jumped off the bed. 'We taught that little ma'moiselle a thing or two, including not to be sick in the boat.' She sighed. 'Nanselow was a different place then. The world was a different place.'

'Will you be coming to the nursery this morning, mamma?'

'If I'm wanted.'

'Of course you're wanted, but I don't want you to do too much.'

'It's boredom that kills, Nancy.'

'I'll send the Land Rover.'

'You'll do no such thing! When I can't walk there I'll stay at home.'

Nancy poured her tea.

'When is Harold going to get another job?'

'I don't know, mamma; he's only just lost this one.'

Ethel shrugged irritably. 'He'll never hold down a job; he's too woolly-minded. Those two are a sad disappointment.'

Nancy said, 'Laura is no problem; she's got her business and she seems to be doing very well at it.'

'Business! Is that what you call it? Selling rubbish to people who are as crazy as she is. You know as well as I do, Nancy, that she's very odd—all this mumbo-jumbo with magic and witchcraft and God-knows what. She'll end up like her mother.'

One difficulty Nancy had foreseen as a second-wife bride of nineteen, was life in the shadow of her predecessor—the 'Rebecca syndrome'—but she need not have worried. With the exception of Laura there was nobody in the Care household who made her feel uncomfortable on that score.

'But she doesn't do anybody any harm, mamma. How she spends her time—'

Ethel cut her short. 'I wish you wouldn't be so damned Christian, Nancy! It's not natural. Sometimes I think you do it just to provoke me into saying what you won't say yourself.'

Perhaps there was a grain of truth in that, for early in her time at Nanselow Nancy had found it advantageous to adopt the role of devil's advocate where the twins and their dead mother were concerned, and she had kept it up.

'That's unfair, mamma.'

The old lady nodded. 'Perhaps it is, but do stop trying to see so much good in people, there isn't that much to see or the world wouldn't be like it is.'

Nancy turned away from the window. 'By the way, Henry asked me to say he's sorry he didn't look in this morning; he was anxious to catch the light—he's painting from the punt again.'

Ethel laughed. 'So he's back to the great out-of-doors. Who is he this time?'

'Isobel says it's a Monet phase coming on.'

'Monet? Wasn't he the chap who ended up painting water lilies? At least that's better than when he thought he was Renoir and we had to pay those fat girls to come in and take their clothes off.'

Nancy said, 'I must go, mamma; see you at the nursery.'

Ethel presented her face to be kissed. 'You're a good girl, Nancy—more of a Care than any of 'em. I only wish it was your John instead of Harold we were looking to to carry on.'

Nancy stiffened angrily. 'You know how I feel about that sort of talk, mamma! It's not fair to Harold, to John, or to me!'

The old lady sighed. 'Yes, yes, I know how you feel. All right, run along.'

The nursery, which Nancy refused to call a garden centre because she grew her own plants, comprised two fields of the original home farm on the western border of the estate. It had been going for five years and as much to Nancy's surprise as other people's it had been a great success though the profits were swallowed by the

13

estate. As the business grew Nancy found herself tied more and more to a desk and paperwork but on this particular morning she allowed herself a couple of hours working alongside Ethel taking cuttings for mist propagation. It was pleasant in the long glass-house with a current of cool air passing through and the smell of plants and soil.

Mostly they worked in silence but she knew that Ethel had something on her mind and it came at last. 'You and Henry . . .'

'What about us?'

'Is everything all right between you?'

'Why shouldn't it be?'

'You know exactly what I mean! Henry is a womanizer; he can't help it, it's in the blood, his father was the same.'

'But he's forty-eight, mamma.'

'What difference does that make? They get worse as they get older. His father was over sixty when he died and he behaved like a randy old billy goat to the last. I should know. I was relieved when Henry married you. Twelve years younger, I thought. She'll keep him out of mischief.'

'And haven't I?'

'I'm not sure. Why don't you sleep with him? Separate beds is one thing but separate rooms—that's quite a different matter.'

There was an edge to Nancy's voice. 'The only reason Henry and I don't sleep in the same room, or the same bed for that matter, is that he snores—like a pig. Does that satisfy you?'

'Not altogether but I suppose you will tell me that it's none of my business. People do that when they don't want to hear the truth. But I'll say this, Henry has that look—it's the sort of look he's had since he was a child whenever he thinks he's getting away with something. If you've got any sense, you'll watch him.'

'I'll bear it in mind.'

Nancy could hardly tell her mother-in-law that she did not much care where Henry found his sexual diversion. She was fond of him and he needed her but she had long since tired of his adolescent sex games.

There was silence in the glasshouse for a while and Nancy hoped that the old lady had said her say but there was more to come.

'There's another thing, while we're talking. I don't think Isobel is pulling her weight. She's my daughter but she's far too ready to settle in some comfortable corner like a pampered cat and let others do the work and the worrying. If she can't earn a decent living at this writing business then she should be helping out in other ways—in the house with Celia or over here with you.'

Nancy spoke primly. 'I think Isobel works hard at her writing and, in any case, she is Henry's sister and that's enough for me, mamma.'

Ethel sighed. 'There's no satisfaction in talking to you, Nancy—none! Why can't you come out with a shot of real old-fashioned venom now and then like anybody else?'

Nancy laughed despite herself.

The mid-day meal at Nanselow was a scratch affair with those who turned up helping themselves to whatever happened to be in the refrigerator. Food reserved for the evening meal was marked with a letter P impaled on a cocktail stick, meaning, 'Prohibited'.

Ethel and Nancy were eating at the nursery; Isobel and Celia shared a tub of cottage cheese and a slice of tinned pineapple followed by a portion of gooey cake and a cup of coffee.

Celia said, 'I think we are in for another instalment of the Gemini saga; she was in his room this morning before she went to work.'

Isobel licked cream from her fingers. 'I thought the Gemini twins were both male—Castor and Pollux.'

Celia ignored her. 'She's getting her claws into him again; bringing him to heel. Sometimes I feel sorry for that boy; he was made to be devoured by women.'

Afterwards Isobel took Cleo for a walk. Cleo was a golden retriever bitch, getting long in the tooth and sedate in deportment so that she and Isobel could wander amicably through the countryside, neither unduly constrained by the other. They walked through the park in the direction of the creek but half-way there they turned off through East Wood, climbing the slopes of the valley's flank along a narrow broken track which suffered with each winter's rain.

The woods were at their best, with a canopy of fresh green overhead and drifts of bluebells like mist on the ground. Every now and then Isobel glimpsed the river through the trees and once she heard the clank of the chain ferry on its way across. Cleo foraged half-heartedly, more from a sense of duty than inclination.

At a point where the trees were thickest Isobel was startled by a sudden commotion close at hand and a massive figure broke out of the undergrowth with a snapping of twigs. Cleo cringed and growled. Dippy Saunders appeared, son of one of Henry's tenant farmers, a hulking youth who pretended to be more stupid than he was.

He stood in the path and looked at Isobel with a sheepish grin. 'I 'ope I never started you, Miss Isobel.'

'No, Dippy, you didn't, but what are you doing here, anyway?'

His eyes wandered over the surrounding scrub. 'I looking for Smutty, our cat, she wandering off.'

'What have you done with your gun?'

The brown eyes widened. 'I don't 'ave no gun up 'ere, Miss Isobel, Sir 'Enry wouldn' like it.'

'No, he wouldn't, so you'd better find it and take it home with you.'

Dippy grinned and stood aside to let her pass.

The path skirted the hump of a broad promontory then dived steeply to a lane which turned inland and eventually joined the road from the ferry. The lane led past Piper's Cottage which had been a gamekeeper's cottage but had been empty for years. Now, as part of NEMP it had been modernized for letting during the summer months and the first tenants were due in a fortnight. Farther along the lane, Tresean, a larger house belonging to the estate, stood in its own grounds screened from the lane by beech trees. Tresean was let on a long lease to Timothy Payne, a man in his forties, who lived there alone.

Isobel and Cleo turned in at the gate of Tresean and walked up the drive which was spongy with a carpet of last year's beech leaves. The house was built of timber in the style of a Swiss chalet, a whim of a nineteenth century Care, and Henry had been fortunate in his tenant who, without obligation, was willing to spend a lot of money on maintenance.

The rattle of a typewriter came through the french windows on the ground floor. Isobel crossed the patch of rough grass in front of the house and with Cleo at her heels entered the room without invitation. It was a large room with bookshelves half-way up the walls and pictures above. The floor was carpeted but there was little furniture; a desk at which Payne had been working, a large round walnut table littered with scholarly periodicals in three or four languages and two or three comfortable armchairs.

'Isobel! I was hoping you would come.'

Payne was tall and thin, with a hatchet face and a mop of unruly hair which had once been dark but was turning grey, a middle-aged Bertrand Russell. He had grey, slightly protuberant eyes and a rather shy, hesitant smile.

Isobel believed that she was his only regular visitor. They had become acquainted through a chance meeting when they were both walking in the woods and another encounter at his gate when she happened to be passing with Cleo.

'Come in and join me for a cup of tea . . .' His approach had been shy and tentative yet when she was leaving after her first visit she had been amused by his strictly conditional offer of future hospitality. 'Do come in whenever you happen to be passing—any afternoon between three and four.' Then, realizing that this might have sounded churlish, he excused but did not modify his terms, 'I'm afraid that I'm a creature of habit; unless I discipline myself to a strict routine I get nothing done.'

She had been calling on him a couple of times a week for three years. She knew that he had once held a post in a university, that he was writing a book on the German philosophers of the Romantic Movement and he had admitted that he was under no constraint to earn a living.

He pulled up a chair for her. 'I'll make the tea.'

Their relationship was guileless and gentle; they never argued or laughed but discussed and smiled. They were like two characters from a Jean Effel cartoon, two doves cooing softly at each other. He made her seem more intelligent than she was or knew herself to be, and in his company she relaxed, becoming more gentle, amenable, softer than others who knew her would have believed possible. At Tresean she never smoked.

After a little while he came back with a tray, tea and biscuits, and they settled down to talk while Cleo sprawled across the doorway like a crumpled skin rug. Isobel returned a book she had borrowed, Eichendorff's *Memoirs of a Good-for-Nothing*.

'What did you think of it?'

Isobel took her time as she always did in answering his questions. 'I suppose charming is an overworked word but I think it fits in this case.'

He smiled. 'A nice bit of escapism, isn't it?'

'Are all his tales so inconsequential?'

He did not answer directly. 'I'd like you to read *Das Schloss Durande* but I don't know if it's available in translation. How's your German?'

'Rusty; but I'd like to try it.'

'You'll find it very different.'

While they talked she had been picking at the nail of the index finger of her left hand.

'What's the matter with your finger?'

'I've split the nail.'

'Let me look . . . I'll trim it for you.' He pulled open a drawer of his desk in which there were boxes of clips, staples and pins as well as a paper knife and a pair of scissors. These were at the front of the drawer but he had opened it far enough for her to see the butt of a gun.

'Tim! You've got a gun. Why on earth . . . ?'

He looked both guilty and contrite. 'It belonged to my father who was an army man.' He pulled the drawer wide. 'It's his service revolver. I should have handed it in when he died but I kept putting it off. To be honest, I've been hoping they would have another of those amnesties they've had in the past.'

Isobel stared at the glinting bluish steel; she felt about guns as she felt about snakes, fascinated and repelled; so much capacity for harm packed in so small a space. 'I think you should get rid of it, Tim. Surely, if it belonged to your father they can't complain about you handing it in?'

'After all these years they might think I've taken my time about it.' He smiled, 'Anyway, I'll do something.'

'Promise?'

She was treated to another twisted smile. 'Promise.'

He snipped off the fragment of nail and put the scissors back in the drawer.

The proper ritual for a visit was clearly understood and carefully observed by both of them. Payne put the cups and saucers back on the tray and stood up; it was a signal. She followed him out into the little hall and up the stairs with their fantastically carved banisters. His bedroom had a sloping timbered ceiling supported by fretted beams which must have harboured the dust of years, and there was a double bed with carved ends, part of the original furniture which would have done justice to mad King Ludwig himself.

They undressed like a long-married couple with no shyness; his lean sinewy body contrasted with her rich plumpness. They lay together and kissed, then with gentleness and little protestations of pleasure and mutual consideration, they made love.

'Sorry . . .'

'I'm not hurting you?'

'No, of course not . . .' Two koala bears could hardly have achieved a more amiable congress.

For Isobel the best part was when they lay side by side afterwards. The sun shone outside but the room, with all its dark varnished woodwork, was like a cool, dim cave with the window at its mouth. She could see the interlacing foliage of two beech trees, brilliantly green, and a wedge of blue sky.

'How are things at Nanselow?'

'Just the same. My nephew—Harold—Henry's son by his first wife, is home. He got the sack from his job in London.'

'Yes, Laura told me that her brother was coming home; she was looking forward to it.'

'*Laura?* When did you see Laura?' Isobel was startled.

'Oh, she's been coming here recently; she discovered that I have a collection of books on occultism and magic which belonged to my mother.'

'You need to be careful, Tim. She's dangerous.' As soon as she had spoken she realized that what she had said must have sounded absurd. He was resting on one elbow, looking down at her.

He smiled. 'Dangerous? Surely not!'

The serpent had found its way into her garden. 'I admit that she can be very engaging with her apparent innocent candour and naivety, but it's a front, Tim . . .'

Whatever she said now he would be sure to attribute to jealousy.

'I'm only telling you this because she's a born trouble-maker.'

Payne chuckled. 'Strange! Do you know of whom she reminded me?'

'No.' Neither did she want to know; she did not want to talk about Laura.

'Of Bettina von Arnim. You remember what von Arnim wrote of his young wife? "Half witch, half angel; half seeress, half liar; half child, half actress; half something-I can't-remember, half nun; half sleepwalker, half coquette."' Payne grinned down at her. 'Of course, von Arnim was more than half joking.'

'Well, I fancy that would flatter Laura and I'm not joking at all.'

He squeezed her thigh and they talked of other things until, by his silence, she realized that it was time for her to go. They dressed and went downstairs. Cleo roused herself from sun-drenched sleep and followed Isobel in a daze. Payne came to the gate to see them off.

Isobel had made no secret of her visits to Tresean but she was sure that no-one suspected that their relationship went further than friendly conversation and the borrowing of books. From her schooldays she had been regarded as belonging to a neuter gender and she preferred it that way.

*

'But what did Harold do, exactly?' So many things puzzled John that his features seemed to express a permanent interrogative.

Alice stared down at the bottle-green water which dimly reflected her fragmented image, familiar yet strange. The dinghy glided up-river with the tide, helped by the lightest of breezes. John drooped over the tiller, long and loose limbed, in one of the more awkward stages of adolescence, while Alice had crossed the threshold from gawky girl to attractive young woman. She trailed her fingers in the water and saw her features dissolve in its rippling wake.

'I think he got some money by faking his expenses.'

'But why?'

'I suppose, because he needed the money.'

'But he must have known—'

'That it was wrong, that he would be found out, that he would probably be sacked if he was—yes, I expect he knew all that but I don't suppose he sat down and worked it out.' As so often, Alice was exasperated by John's tiresome logic. 'I'm not defending what he did but people do sometimes do things without thinking about it for a month beforehand—at least most people do.'

John said, 'I hope he doesn't stay long, he spoils things.'

'He's as much right here as any of us; more than me.'

'I'm not talking about his rights.'

Alice sighed. 'Look! There's a heron—over there on the mud below that alder.'

But John was not to be deflected. 'He doesn't feel the same about Nanselow as we do.'

'No, I don't expect he does. We all know the place is going to ruin and it will be his problem one day, not ours.'

John laughed unexpectedly, transforming his earnest features, 'In fact, I expect it will be a hostel for the Youth of the Red Banner or a convalescent home for workers of the People's Republic.'

Alice combed her dark hair with her fingers; it was limp, wet with sea water. She was a beautiful girl, on the way to being a beautiful woman.

'When you think of it, Harold hasn't spent much time here, has he? He was only nine when they sent him to boarding school, then there was that business college in London, then his job.'

John said, 'I'm glad father didn't send me to boarding school.'

'He couldn't have afforded to anyway; the twins went because they were paid for out of the money their mother left.' Alice frequently talked to John as an adult to a child.

Nanselow lay straight ahead, set in sloping parkland, flanked by gardens and backed by trees. The fourth baronet had hidden the old Georgian house behind a façade of post-Puginite Gothic, giving it an air of zany fantasy appropriate to a family whose motto was *Somniare audete*, Dare to dream.

The brimming river, the still trees growing almost to the water's edge, and the pale blue cloudless sky combined to create a scene of utter tranquillity.

'God! I wish something would happen.' Alice spoke almost in a whisper because she was speaking to herself.

John looked at her with concern. 'Aren't you happy, Alice?'

'Should I be?'

'I think so; you've no real reason not to be, have you?'

'Haven't I?' She was caustic. 'I don't really know. I'll write down a list of all the pros and cons, add them up and subtract one from the other and let you know.'

They were nearing the shore and John began to raise the drop keel.

'I feel I want to break out—*do* something.'

'Another fortnight or so and your A-levels will be over, then—'

She cut him short angrily. 'Christ! How you sound like my mother. What do I care about school and A-levels and university or any other damn thing?'

John was worried and mystified. 'You've said things like that before, do you really mean them?'

'Of course I mean them!'

'Then what do you really want?'

She looked towards the house and was silent for a while. 'I want something to happen—anything. Anything that takes hold of me and makes me do something whether I want to or not. I want to live; can't you understand that?'

John shook his head.

'I didn't think you would; you wouldn't recognize life if you met it in the street unless it had a label round its neck. Then you would want to study it through your binoculars.'

Laura's room had a large window facing west towards the plantation, a mixed stand of hardwood trees planted by Henry's grandfather to replace losses to the timber control in the first war.

It was a strange room with no chairs, only cushions of great variety in size, shape and colour, and a Japanese folding bed. There were mirrors at floor level; the walls were hung with un-framed prints, scrolls, texts and charts. The curtains were embroidered with zodiacal signs and Tattwas symbols and part of one wall was taken up with a fully coloured mural of the Rose Cross. Below the cross there was a wall mirror and a very low wooden table like an altar. On the table was a framed text of Aleister Crowley's notorious dictum, 'Do what thou wilt shall be the whole of the law', picked out in red and gilt letters. The text was flanked by two brass censers in which joss sticks burned, and propped against the table was a large card bearing the sub-Tattwas symbol, Tejas of Prithivi—the fiery aspect of earth—a yellow square enclosed by a red equilateral triangle.

Laura had been introduced to occult studies by her mother's sister, her aunt Lucille. Lucille had married a Parisian business-man with a lot of money and the good sense to die young so that Lucille had been left a very rich widow. Laura had always spent part of her school vacations in Paris with her aunt and when she left school she had gone there for an indefinite stay; in fact it was assumed that she would settle there for good, but eighteen months ago she had turned up at Nanselow with her baggage and shortly afterwards started the shop.

Laura sat on a cushion in the lotus position, facing the low table, the mirror and the Tattwas symbol. She wore a plain white robe and she had removed her spectacles. A cassette player made electronic music in very slow time. Her body swayed almost imperceptibly but her gaze remained fixed on the Tattwas card.

She had held this position for about fifteen minutes. At first she was distracted by tension in her leg muscles, by acute discomfort in her ankles, by the effort to maintain a straight back, by a slight current of air across her face, by the tickling of her hair against her forehead . . .

But she knew that all this would pass, that it would be followed by a dull ache which would creep up through her thighs and invade her whole body, then it would vanish. After that she would be free, her body would cease to trouble her and her whole mind would be focused through her seeing eyes.

The minutes passed, the pain came and spread through her limbs and body and disappeared. Her eyes saw the Tattwas symbol with absolute clarity for the first time; it seemed to be suspended in the air within a few inches of her face; the shapes took on depth and became three-dimensional; they duplicated themselves and merged again several times and finally lost all form so that her vision was filled with a misty orange glow. The colour faded and the mist cleared.

There was a tapping at the door but Laura was oblivious. After a moment or two the door opened and Harold came in. He looked at his sister then closed the door and sat on a cushion, his back to the wall, to wait. He waited a quarter-of-an-hour during which Laura remained all but motionless, her eyes open but unseeing, her hands clasped in repose. The cassette player made electronic music, strange inharmonious chords sustained until the limit of tolerance seemed to be near, then abruptly broken off.

Laura stirred; she sighed deeply and shivered, then drew her robe about her. Her first glance round the room was vague and uncomprehending, then she got slowly to her feet. She picked up her glasses and put them on.

'Oh, there you are! I thought you'd forgotten or decided not to come.'

'But I've been sitting here, waiting.'

'Never mind.' She seemed to recover her usual grace and freedom of movement very quickly. She placed cushions and they sat shoulder to shoulder, their backs to the wall. The resemblance between them was striking. Had they been of the same sex they could easily have passed for identical twins, but the features which gave Laura's face a delicate strength made Harold appear somewhat effeminate; Peter Pan grown up.

They remained silent for a time, listening to the tape, then Harold said, 'What happened to Bach?'

'Oh, I left Bach behind; this electronic music is so much more evocative. I wish I'd found it sooner; it was pure chance, a tape I happened to hear in Truro. Lucille had finished with Bach too but she has gone over to plainsong; I tried it but the atmosphere it produces is too monastic.' She broke off. 'I've been with mother.'

'With *mother*?'

'Oh, not across the great divide!' She laughed. 'Not yet, anyway. Just back to when we were children. I've found that by really disciplined concentration on the Tattwas symbols I can recover lost memories—even memories of very early childhood. You know the sort of thing they can do under hypnosis. I can re-live bits of the past in a dream-like way; I suppose it's a kind of self-hypnosis.'

Harold was always astonished by his sister's enthusiasms and baffled by her self-confidence; she never seemed to have doubts and when he was with her he felt flabby and aimless.

From a sense of duty he asked, 'What did you remember this time?'

'We were on the grass down by the creek, mother, father, you and I. I had discovered a new game I could play by myself. All I had to do was to stare at a place where the sun was shining on the water, then close my eyes and open them again a tiny bit. I could see hundreds of stars and if I moved my eyelids the stars would dance and jump about.'

'Was that all?'

'No, you were playing some distance away, under the trees where there were lots of twigs lying about and you were arranging the bits of wood in a pattern. I walked towards you, sliding my bare feet through the grass as if I were skating, and when I came close I saw that you had made a picture of a house out of the twigs with

25

windows, doors and chimneys. I kept on walking, dragging my feet so that all your bits of wood were kicked away.'

'I remember that.'

'Do you? I didn't until I recalled it just now in trance. But doesn't that prove that it works?' She turned to him with shining eyes. 'Do you remember what happened afterwards?'

'No.'

'Mother saw what I had done and she came running over; she picked me up and slapped me very hard on both thighs.' Laura massaged her thighs through her robe. 'I can still feel the sting in those slaps. Father called out, "Deborah! Deborah! I don't think the child meant to do it, it was an accident." But I didn't want him to interfere, it was something between mother and me.'

'I don't remember about mother slapping you.'

'No? Anyway, that's enough about me. What about you? This is the first time we've really had a chance to talk since you came back.'

'I got the sack.'

'I know that, but why?'

'For fiddling my expenses. I was short of money and—'

'But didn't you go to Uncle Joe?'

'It was Uncle Joe who sacked me.'

'How wretchedly spiteful of him! But if it means that you will be home then I'm glad.'

'I shall have to get another job, Laura; there's nothing for me here.'

'But why do you have to get another job? You won't starve. Mother's money is enough for one—just about, and I don't need any of it.'

'I have to do something with my life, Laura.'

Laura reached up and stroked his hair. 'Poor boy, your life is here. The house, everything will be yours one day; the others are just . . . just parasites.'

Harold was disturbed. 'I don't think you can call them that. I mean, they can't help being here any more than we can.'

Laura's face hardened. 'They hate us, Harold. But whatever

you think of them there's no reason why you shouldn't stay here as I do.'

'It's different for you, Laura.'

'Why is it different?'

'Partly because you are a woman, I suppose; but apart from that you've got the shop.'

The cassette tape ran out and the music came to an abrupt stop leaving a silence like a vacuum.

Harold said, 'Why did you come back, Laura? Weren't you happier in Paris with Aunt Lucille?'

'Yes, I was happier, but I came back because I was determined not to let them get away with it.'

Harold frowned. 'But who is getting away with what?'

Laura raised her thin shoulders. 'I don't want to talk about it now.' She stood up in a single effortless movement, 'Stay where you are.'

When Harold was away he could think of his sister's more bizarre activities as a sort of game she played; part of an interesting role in which she had cast herself, but when he was with her he almost believed.

She put on a fresh tape which began with sounds like marbles rolling downstairs in agonizingly slow motion. Then she returned to the cushion beside him.

'Unbutton your shirt.'

He did as he was told; she took off her glasses and slid one arm round his shoulders, looking into his eyes and smiling. With the fingers of her free hand she began to trace delicate patterns on his chest.

'Relax! You are full of guilt. Let it drain away through my fingers. Don't you know that guilt is the enemy of life?'

Chapter Two

LAURA DID NOT open her shop on Thursdays and on Thursday morning she walked across the park and through the woods to Tresean. It was a fresh morning, overnight rain still dripped from the trees and there was mud underfoot but the sun shone from a clear blue sky. Unlike Isobel, Laura had not been assigned a time for her visits; she walked up the drive and drifted through the french windows to find the room empty except for Payne's tabby cat asleep on his desk in a patch of sunshine.

Laura wore tight jeans and a cornflower blue shirt which she knew set off the gold of her hair; a contrived casualness. When Payne came in she was looking at his pictures. He was startled by her and obviously embarrassed. A whitish stubble sprouted on his chin and he wore a dirty grey cardigan and slacks.

'Laura! I haven't even shaved.'

She did not trouble to turn round. 'I've been looking at your pictures.'

He came to stand beside her. 'That one is by Friedrich—Caspar David Friedrich. Many of his pictures are like that—looking out from darkness into light. Trees or cliffs or the walls of a room form a dark frame for a brilliantly lit landscape, and often there are pensive, enigmatic figures who seem to be looking out with you.'

'The individual exploring the universe.'

'Yes.' He was pleased by her understanding. 'But for Friedrich, as for all the German Romantics, it was a reciprocal process, by exploring ourselves we come to know the universe and by exploring the universe we come to know ourselves.'

She turned her eyes and her spectacles on him. 'I came to borrow *Transcendental Magic* if you will lend it.'

'Of course! You know where it is.' He was disconcerted by her abrupt change of subject. She never allowed him to really talk to her, to show her something of himself. 'You are welcome to all my books on occultism, Laura. I've told you before; since my mother died they have never been used.'

'I'll borrow Levi.' She picked out the book from the shelves and put it on his desk. The round lenses confronted him again, neutralizing the expression of her eyes so that her gaze seemed enigmatic. 'Do you think that ritual magic can be effective, Tim?'

He smiled his lecturer's smile. 'That's a short question which opens up a very large subject.'

She perched herself on the edge of his desk and sank her fingers into the cat's fur, massaging its body; the cat rolled over and stretched its front paws. She said, 'Really? It seems simple enough to me. All I want to know is whether you believe that it is possible to discover anything about the past or the future or to influence people's lives through ritual magic.'

He smiled again then remembered his stubbly chin and placed his hand in front of his mouth. 'Answer yes or no. But I can't. My answer is that I think it could be. Do you want me to explain?'

'If you like.' She was indifferent.

'Well, the human psyche operates at two levels, the one conscious and rational, the other unconscious and irrational. It is the second which is dominant when we dream or enter a state of trance. At that level, it may be that we have access to sources of knowledge and even of power, not recognized by our conscious minds. One just does not know.'

He was pleased by his cleverness and awaited her approval but she seemed wholly absorbed in playing with the cat. He went on, dashed: 'Probably the ceremonies of ritual magic are mere recipes for freeing the unconscious from the fetters of the rational mind, a means of inducing a trance-like condition and concentrating one's energies to a desired end.

'The recipes in the grimoires, re-hashed by Levi, Mathers and the rest, are bizarre but, for some people, they may work.' He smiled, 'They may "turn you on" and that is probably what it is all about.

No doubt other, simpler recipes would work as well or better; the essential requirement is that they produce a very high level of emotional commitment, an orgasmic concentration of the whole being.'

Laura said, 'I see. So you think that it is essentially sexual.'

'No, not necessarily; all I have said is that in order for any of these rituals to have a chance of working one has to achieve the same degree of emotional concentration and commitment as in sexual orgasm.'

She said again, 'I see.'

She slid off his desk and picked up the book she was to borrow. The cat jumped to the floor and padded away. They were standing very close to each other.

Payne said, 'If you are going in for ritual magic, you had better take Crowley; his instructions are explicit if sometimes impracticable.'

She said, coldly, 'I've got Crowley. Well, I'll let you know how I get on.'

Although this was an obvious preliminary to leaving she made no move but stood, looking up at him through her spectacles then, abruptly, she took them off. It seemed to be an intimate gesture, a signal, perhaps an invitation. He put his arms round her and drew her to him; he pressed his lips against hers regardless of the stubble on his chin and his tongue sought entry to her mouth. One hand slipped under her shirt and explored the prominent vertebrae and firm muscles of her back. At first she was entirely passive then the book she was holding fell to the floor and she began to push him away with small hard hands.

'That's enough, Tim!'

He released her, embarrassed. 'I'm sorry . . .'

She pulled down her shirt, unzipped her jeans and tucked it in with the greatest composure. 'I thought I'd better stop you; screwing two women in the same family would be rather much, don't you think?' She picked up the book from the floor, put on her glasses, and with a sweep of her hand restored her hair to order.

'I don't know what you are talking about.'

'No?' She smiled. 'One thing you should know about me, Tim—I find out everything sooner or later.'

He walked with her to the drive gate. 'I hope this won't keep you away.' He was pathetically humble.

'Why should it?'

The evening meal on Fridays was special, it was known as 'dinner' instead of the 'supper' of other days. It was supposed to be a time of relaxed togetherness and participation was all but mandatory. The instigator was Ethel who claimed to be following an old tradition and even Laura would not lightly run the gauntlet of the old lady's displeasure. Altogether it was an excuse for mild extravagance.

Celia made a special effort with the food and Isobel helped; Nancy came back early from the nursery to do her share. The ritual of the occasion was important; the three women drank sherry in the kitchen while they made the final preparations; John and Alice set the table; Henry saw to the wine, and carved. He sat at the head of the table and Ethel at the foot, the others sat where fancy took them.

They ate in the dining-room instead of the little breakfast-room where they usually had their evening meal. The dining-room retained much of its original charm and elegance. The oriental wallpaper with its pattern of cranes and bamboos was intact, though faded; the furniture included a Sheraton sideboard, a set of Hepplewhite chairs and a corner cupboard which displayed a Worcester dinner service decorated with exotic birds. There were family portraits on the walls including one attributed to Reynolds. Henry called it his strong room.

Nancy thought, But how long can it go on? It was not only a question of how long they could continue to pay the bills and keep the place in some semblance of habitability, but how long would enough of them have the will to try? For Henry, these questions hardly seemed to arise, he spoke of Harold succeeding him at Nanselow as though the continuance of the Care family there was part of some immutable design removed from the hazards of time and chance. Faced with an unpleasant reality he took refuge with his paints and his gardening. Or so it seemed.

John sat next to Ethel, explaining to her about bodies and slips, glazes and firing temperatures. John was taking pottery lessons at school and learning to use his hands in new and satisfying ways. Dear, good John! He had inherited Nancy's looks, the dark hair and eyes, the pale skin and sensitive lips. Sometimes she wondered about the sources of his patience, his even temper and mole-like industry.

Alice sat on the other side of the old lady, next to Harold, who was next to his sister and, therefore, silent. Nancy thought, Alice has become a woman and a very attractive one, exceptionally intelligent, but volatile and unpredictable. A flutter on the Glittering Prizes Stakes is all very well but what mother would not settle for less promise and fewer perils? Nancy wondered what manner of man had bequeathed such talents to his unknown daughter. Celia had never mentioned him and even Isobel, for whom there were few secrets, sometimes referred to Alice as the virgin birth.

At another level Nancy was talking to Celia about the demand for bedding plants.

Celia watched her daughter and wished with painful intensity that she understood her.

Isobel sat next to her brother. Theirs was an uneasy relationship and every now and then Henry's rather foolish laugh, an explosive burst, like a cork popping out of a bottle, betrayed his nervousness.

Harold and Laura scarcely exchanged a word but the others were prepared to believe that they communicated by subtler means. Henry watched them with deep seated unease and a sense of guilt. Laura was the double of what her mother had been when he married her. Looking at Laura it was inevitable that he should recall those first weeks and months of marriage when he believed that he had tapped an inexhaustible well of passion and eroticism. And Harold—Harold was so much like his sister that Henry was disturbed when he saw them together, disturbed as he sometimes was by an ill-timed smutty joke. He moved irritably in his chair.

'You're starving yourself, Laura! For heaven's sake, Harold, get your sister to eat something; she'll make herself ill.'

Harold looked round the table and thought. These people are my family yet I hardly know them.

While Nancy was serving dessert Laura began to talk, drawing everyone's attention. 'I've seen Tim Payne several times recently; isn't he a strange man?' She took an apple from the basket Nancy offered and started to peel it, holding it with the tips of her long fingers as though performing an act of great delicacy. 'He's got a collection of books on occult subjects which belonged to his mother, a very valuable collection actually. He wanted to give them to me but of course I couldn't take them though I'm glad of the chance to refer to them.'

A thin riband of peel came off in a continuous coil. 'Did you know that he has a mistress?' She looked round with an expression of vague inquiry. 'I always thought he was some kind of hermit; a modern St Anthony with only his erotic thoughts to keep him company, but there is a real flesh-and-blood woman though I've no idea who she is.'

The colour rose and enveloped Isobel's freckles; Laura's gaze turned on her for only a fraction of a second, but long enough.

The apple peeled, Laura proceeded to cut it into sections and the operation seemed to involve all her attention. When it was done, she went on, 'He's got a gun, too.'

'A gun?' Henry looked at his daughter, mystified as he often was by her apparent inconsequence. 'What's wrong with that? I had several until . . . well, until things started to go wrong.'

Laura said, 'You are talking about shot-guns, father; Tim has a revolver.'

'Left over from the war.'

'Tim isn't old enough to have been in the war.'

Henry became peevish. 'His father then. What does it matter?'

'I simply wondered why he needs to keep a revolver in a drawer of his desk.'

*

33

After the meal Harold went off to spend the rest of the evening with a former school friend. It was after midnight when he returned and the family had gone to bed, but Laura's door was open and she called to him.

She was sitting up in her floor-bed which was covered with a duvet embroidered with mystical signs. In the soft light from her bedside lamp her skin gave the illusion of transparency and her golden hair shone like a crown. Her arms were bare and her hands rested on a lacquered box, the hands of a Balinese dancer. She was not wearing her glasses.

'Did you have a nice evening?'

'Not bad.' It might have seemed disloyal to be more enthusiastic.

'Did you drink a lot?'

'Only a beer or two.'

'You shouldn't drink, Harold. Alcohol clouds the mind and destroys the brain. Are you in a hurry to get to bed?'

He said, reluctantly, 'I'm not all that tired.'

'Then close the door and come and sit by me.'

He did as he was told.

'Was I in your mind this evening?'

'Yes.' It was true, to such an extent that his friend probably thought him poor company.

Laura smiled. 'I willed you to think of me; I was thinking of you and I had these to help me.' She raised the lid of the lacquered box and started to take the things out, one at a time. The first was a piece of costume jewellery in the form of a swallow enclosed in a circlet of plated metal. 'Do you remember that?'

'It was a dare.' He remembered it all too vividly.

'My very first dare; you took it from Woolworth's and brought it home to me. I told you exactly which of the pieces I wanted. Do you remember?'

'Of course I remember.'

'And this?'

He nodded. It was a lipstick. 'That came from a shop in Wharf Lane.'

34

'You even got the right colour.'

'But you never used it.'

'Of course not, silly! These things were symbols, not for use.' She reached into the box once more and came out with a fountain pen. Each object had a little label attached showing the date. 'I'm sure you haven't forgotten this one.'

'Old Acker's fountain pen. There was hell to pay when he missed it.' Ackermann had taught German at Harold's school.

'You hated him, didn't you?'

'He was a bastard to me.'

Even now he had not the courage to tell her that of all her so-called dares, the pen was the only one he had actually stolen, the others he had bought with his meagre pocket money.

'And not long after you brought me the pen Ackermann became ill, didn't he?'

'He had a stroke or something; they said that he was paralysed all down one side and that he couldn't talk properly.' He looked at his sister in sudden astonishment. 'You're not saying . . . Laura, for heaven's sake!'

She placed her hand over his. 'It's better not to speak of it.'

They were silent for a while, hands touching. Then she said, 'You and I are one, Harold; ours is the closest friendship that is possible between two human beings; we grew together in the same womb. Think what that means; there can be no closer intimacy.'

Harold was disturbed by the images her words brought to his mind, he found them distasteful but dared not show it and tried to sound tolerantly objective. 'I suppose identical twins are even closer.'

'Nonsense! They are two, mere carbon copies of each other; neither together nor separate do they make a whole as we do. We are the complement one of the other, male and female, positive and negative, active and passive, the yang dragon and the yin vase.' She ran her hand through his fair curls. 'Apollo and Artemis.' As she said this she smiled so sweetly that he was moved.

'You are a witch!'

'Of course.' She laughed.

35

But Harold was uneasy and wanted to get away. The grandfather clock on the landing growled and struck one.

'Time I was in bed.'

'No—wait!' She put out a restraining hand. 'We are our mother's children, Harold.'

He laughed nervously. 'Father's too, I hope.'

'I'm serious; there is nothing of that man in either of us. Do you remember mother clearly, Harold?'

'Yes, I think so. After all, we were six when she died.'

Laura smiled and her eyes lost focus as though gazing on things unseen by others. Harold was never sure when his sister was genuinely moved or when she was pretending to be in order to make some point.

'I remember her so *vividly*! I can see her bending over me when she came in to tuck us up at night. She looked so beautiful I could hardly believe that she was real. I used to tell myself that she was not really our mother but a fairy who looked after us. She was twenty-six when she died.' Laura turned her gaze on him. 'What do you remember of her, Harold?'

'Mostly the quarrels she had with father. I would wake up in the night and hear her shouting at him—screaming sometimes. I used to lie in bed, stiff and trembling, longing for it to be over.' Harold shuddered. 'It was horrible!'

Laura smiled. 'Poor boy! I remember the quarrels too but I see now that they were his fault; he was to blame.'

'Father? I don't see how you make that out. Aunt Isobel says that she led him a hell of a life.'

'Isobel!' Laura was contemptuous. 'Just think: he married mother when she was nineteen—a young vivacious girl tied to a stupid and insensitive man. I can imagine what she went through.'

Harold was piqued. 'I think you are being unfair, Laura! I don't see father as either stupid or insensitive and he was only six years older than mother.'

As always, when there were signs of an argument, Laura changed the subject. 'Do you remember mother's death?'

'Yes, of course I do.'

'I mean, do you remember the actual day when it happened?'

He hesitated, anxious not to get it wrong. 'I think so. Father came into our nursery, very red in the face. You were there. He sat in the window-seat and called us over and put his arms round us . . .'

'Yes?'

'He said, "Your mother has had a very bad accident." I can't remember exactly what he said after that but I know that he told us she had fallen from the Prospect Tower.'

'Where were you when it happened?'

This was the kind of test Laura had often put him through when they were children and he still recalled with uneasiness her withering contempt when he failed to make the grade.

'I don't know when it happened.'

'It was in the afternoon; where were you that afternoon?'

'I can't remember; after all, we were only kids and it was sixteen years ago.'

'I remember. We were on Bar Beach with Aunt Isobel. We were throwing flat stones into the water and trying to make them skim. Do you remember now?'

Harold had to admit that he did not.

'It was very hot and I got bored with throwing stones so I wandered off across the rocks to where I could see the ferry and I watched it cross with a load of cars. People were hanging over the rails taking photographs and I remember some of them waved to me.'

Harold said, 'Do you remember all that or is it . . . ?' He glanced across at the low table.

She answered shortly, 'Of course I remember. Anyway, from where I was standing watching the ferry I could look up and see the Prospect Tower coming out above the trees. From down there on the rocks it looked an enormous height and there were people on the top. I could see mother in her orange dress, and father was wearing that ridiculous white hat of his, and Nancy—'

'*Nancy?*'

37

'Yes, Nancy was there.'

'But that was before mother died.'

'Of course it was, but Nancy used to come here then, don't you remember?'

Harold's memories were vague but he agreed, 'Yes, I suppose she did.'

Laura had her 'seeing' look, 'Mother was standing in one of the slots of the battlements, looking down—I can see her perfectly plainly in my mind—and I think father was behind her, sort of reaching out . . .'

Laura passed a hand in front of her eyes. 'It was hot—very hot, and looking up made me feel giddy. The tower seemed to move, I suppose it was the shimmering heat.'

Harold was astonished to see little beads of perspiration on his sister's forehead.

'It was then that it must have happened, Harold—while I was standing there.'

'But it couldn't have done; you didn't see anything.'

She shook her head. 'No, I don't suppose I did. I don't know.'

Harold was deeply moved; he reached out his hand and touched her arm.

Saturday morning. Laura had gone to work, Harold and Alice were still in bed, John had gone off somewhere with his binoculars, bird-watching, and Henry was out on the estate. As usual at this time the three women were in the kitchen.

Celia brushed crumbs from the table on to a plate. 'What was all that in aid of last night?'

Isobel said nothing and Nancy did not look up from the paper she was reading. 'All what?'

'Laura's talk about Tim Payne having a woman. Do you think it's true? I've always assumed he was a bit the other way.'

Nancy knew that Celia had not missed Laura's glance at Isobel any more than she had herself. Celia was stirring for trouble. Nancy sighed; she seemed to spend half her life trying to stop the holes in a colander. 'You know what Laura is; she says that sort of thing for the sake of saying it.'

But Celia was not so easily put off. 'She must have something to go on. I must say, it surprises me; I've never had more than six words out of the man in all the years he's been there. You should know, Isobel, you must have some idea of what goes on.'

Isobel crushed out her cigarette. 'You, Celia, are as bad as that little vixen last night. I've made no secret of the fact that I look in on Tim Payne occasionally; we chat over a cup of tea and he lends me books. Only someone with a peculiar mind would try to make more of it than that.'

'I've never suggested—'

But Isobel would not listen, she got up and went out, slamming the door behind her.

Celia knew that she had gone too far, that she had transgressed the rules of brinkmanship. 'I'm sure I don't care if she sleeps with Payne every day of the week and twice on Sundays.'

Nancy folded her newspaper. 'Then why bring it up?' She set about preparing Ethel's breakfast tray.

Celia collected the dirty dishes and started to wash up; she also made an effort to restore normal relations, at least with Nancy. 'Since Laura came home from Paris it's been just like having Deborah back again. Talk about mother and daughter! Sometimes it's uncanny.'

Nancy was cool. 'I wouldn't know about that. Naturally, I wasn't living here then.'

'No, but you were a frequent visitor; you must have had some idea of what was going on. Incidentally, doesn't it ever strike you as a bit odd that it was Deborah who brought you here in the first place?'

Nancy trod carefully. 'It was Deborah who first invited me to Nanselow and it was through her that I got to know you all, but I don't see that as very odd.' Nancy filled a small jug with milk for Ethel. 'For some reason Deborah took a liking to me; I've no idea why. I mean, she was several years older and we hadn't a great deal in common.'

39

'But it wasn't long before you were a regular visitor just the same.'

'I know. I suppose I was flattered by the friendship of an older woman, a woman who was married and very sophisticated like Deborah. In those days too, a standing invitation to Nanselow was still quite a lift for a girl, especially a bank-clerk's daughter.'

'What did your mother think about it?'

'She wasn't too keen. I think she suspected Deborah of being a les.'

'You were a very beautiful young girl.'

'What's that got to do with it? Whatever Deborah was, she wasn't a les.'

Celia started to wipe the dishes she had washed. 'Haven't you ever heard of people who keep a cat just to tease it?'

'Deborah certainly never teased me.'

'No, but she used you to tease Henry. You were bait, Nancy. "Look! This is what you want, isn't it? But you try to get it, old boy!" Looking back, haven't you ever seen it like that?'

'No, I can't say that I have.' Nancy was subdued; she realized that Celia was probably right. She put the kettle on to boil for Ethel's tea. It was odd to see events of the past in such a different light after all those years.

'Don't you remember that she asked you to pose for Henry in the nude?'

'Yes, and I refused.'

'I know, but it makes the point, doesn't it? Henry understood what it was all about. You can look but not touch.'

Celia wiped the dishes for a time in silence. The kettle boiled; Nancy warmed the pot and made tea. One teaspoonful of China, one of Ceylon.

Abruptly, Celia said, 'We've never really talked about Deborah before, have we? I wonder why. It's as if we felt some kind of guilt about her though why we should, God knows. Does Henry ever mention her?'

'No.'

Nancy cut two thin slices of bread and buttered them.

40

'Nancy, there's something I've wanted to ask you for years . . . At the inquest you backed Henry up; you said that you saw her fall.'

'So?'

'Could she have jumped?'

It was some time before Nancy replied and when she did she spoke very quietly. 'I don't really see the point of raking this up now but the truth is that I didn't actually see Deborah fall. I was standing fairly close to Henry and she was on the edge, looking down; she was playing the fool, teasing him in the way she had, half playful, half vicious; but it happened that at the very instant that mattered I was watching Laura—'

'*Laura*! Where does she come into it?'

'She was down on Bar Beach with Harold and Isobel that afternoon and she must have wandered over the rocks to watch the ferry or something. Anyway, she was down there. I can see her now in her little orange briefs with her hair about her shoulders looking up at us. I waved but apparently she didn't see me, at any rate she didn't wave back. It was scorchingly hot and I remember thinking she ought to be wearing something to protect her from sunburn.'

'But that means she must have seen her mother fall.'

'You'd think so, but she obviously didn't. If she had she would have made a fuss—after all, she was six at the time. The first I knew was a shout from Henry and I saw that Deborah wasn't there any more. It was a second or two before I realized what had happened. I shall never forget the look on Henry's face.'

Harold was living in a state of suspense, like a sick man awaiting the results of his tests. Since he had been home only Laura had referred to his lost job but the silence of the others was like a reproach. Soon his father would want that 'little talk'. He had rehearsed the occasion over and over again.

'Let's be sensible about this, Harold—see it in perspective.'

No harsh words, no recriminations, but in the end the question would have to be faced, 'You are still a very young man, Harold; if you had a completely free choice, what would you do?'

41

He had searched his soul for an answer. What would I do? What *would* I do?

'There must be something—something that interests you . . .'

All the others had something; Laura, her shop and her magic; Nancy, her nursery; Isobel, her writing; John, his potting and his woodwork and his natural history . . . I wish . . . But he could not condense a vague longing into words.

'You are drifting, Harold, that's your real trouble,'—his uncle, giving him the sack.

In fact, when he found himself alone with his father, nothing of the kind happened. He was in the stable yard, wondering how best to pass away the time until lunch when his father caught him unawares.

'Oh, there you are! I'm glad I've run into you. I'm on my way to talk to Holiday and I'd like you to come with me if you will.'

For as long as Harold could recall Captain Holiday and Miss Pearl, a lady in her middle fifties who undoubtedly had a surname though no-one remembered what it was, had occupied a large ground-floor room in the estate office behind the stable block, surrounded by black deed-boxes, massive wooden filing cabinets, account books with red-leather bindings, dust and the uniquely pungent odour of Captain Holiday's pipe.

'Ah, Holiday! I've brought Harold along for a chat.'

It always surprised Harold that his father, so diffident with the family, often adopted a brusque and even peremptory manner with outsiders. It particularly impressed him that this should be so with the aristocratic looking Holiday.

'Good morning, Miss Pearl.'

'Good morning, Sir Henry; Good morning, Mr Harold.' Miss Pearl was at work on a forty-year-old Remington, typing letters on estate notepaper which, itself, had turned slightly yellow with age.

Captain Holiday sat at his roll-topped desk amid a litter of paper, his pipe smouldered in an ash-tray which advertised an extinct brand of cigarettes and he watched Henry with slightly nervous expectancy.

'Now that Harold is home, I'm hoping that he won't be in too much hurry to leave us again. It's time he started to learn something about the estate, to work his way in, so to speak.' Henry was standing with his back to the room, looking out of the window. He turned abruptly, 'Don't you think so, Holiday?'

'Yes . . . Yes, I suppose it is.'

'I want him to spend some time with you—a few hours a day, learning the ropes and getting ideas . . . It's ideas this place needs and Harold is not stupid.' Henry turned to his son. 'How does the idea strike you? Are you willing to give it a trial? See how you get on?'

'Well, yes, if that's what you—'

'Good! That's a load off my mind. You'd better find him a desk or something, Holiday . . . It might be an idea to clear out some of this stuff or put him in one of the upstairs rooms . . . Anyway, I leave all that to you.'

Henry walked out into the yard, drawing Harold after him. 'I'm sorry to spring it on you like that, Harold, but often it's the best way. I remember when my father . . . Anyway, things were different then. But I've been thinking along these lines for a long time—before there was any question of you packing in the London job.' He looked round as though confiding a secret and not wishing to be overheard. 'There are real problems in running this place and things won't get any easier, with inflation and a tight money supply. What we've got to do is to plan ahead.'

Henry walked across the yard and propped his behind against an old mounting block. He looked up at the roofs of the house rising above the stables.

'We've lived here for three-and-a-half centuries, Harold, and we're not going to be squeezed out because we're too stupid to learn the rules of the new game. When you've had time to settle in a bit I shall be asking you for ideas.'

Henry broke off and waited to hear his son's reaction but Harold said nothing.

'Well? Is that all right?'

'Yes, if you think—'

'Good! Learn the admin routine from Holiday but don't take too much notice of him outside of that. He's a good chap but he's got the mind of a clerk. No vision. And God knows, what we want now is vision.' Henry grinned up at his son. '*Somniare audete*—with a motto like that it shouldn't be too difficult, should it?'

Harold smiled too, but from a sense of duty. 'No, I suppose not.'

'Go and see Holiday first thing Monday morning. Be prepared to lick stamps or whatever for a bit but not for too long—understand?'

'Well, yes—'

'That's it, then.'

Harold's mind was in a whirl. He saw at once that he had been offered a way of escape which was also a trap. He was both flattered and dismayed. He left the yard, crossed the park, and climbed the steep slope through East Wood, following the path which led to the summit of the promontory and to the folly which was known as the Prospect Tower. The tower had been built by some eighteenth-century Care ancestor; it was a pentagonal building, four stories high, with phoney battlements and an interior spiral staircase. The walls were covered with ivy but the structure was still sound.

Harold came out of the scrub and stood looking up at the tower. It was from those absurd battlements that his mother had fallen sixteen years before. Since then the tower had carried with it a taboo. It was rarely mentioned; it had been placed out-of-bounds to the children after the accident; a lock had been fitted to the door and the ground floor window had been shuttered. Now the lock was broken and the shutters had been carried away in a gale. There was, in fact, no longer a window on the ground floor, only a gap where the window had been.

'Hullo!'

Harold was startled, then he saw Alice, she was sitting in the window space, her back propped against one side, her feet against the other, a book in her lap.

'Having a quiet read?'

She made a wry face and held up the book, *Advanced Level Physics*.

Harold went through the doorway into the ground-floor room. The floor of blue slate slabs looked as though it had been recently swept clean.

'Been cleaning up the old place?'

Alice got down from her perch, brushing the dust from her jeans and massaging her buttocks. 'Not me.'

Harold was looking at the massive stone walls and at the little doorway with its Gothic arch which led to the spiral staircase. 'I wonder what persuaded them to spend money building a place like this.'

'Keeping up with the Joneses, I expect. Every estate worth the name had its folly and this is better than a fake-classical ruin.'

Harold said, 'You've got your A-levels coming off soon, haven't you?'

'Starting when we go back on Monday.'

'From what I've heard it should be a walk-over.'

Alice gave a little yelp. 'You must be joking!'

'What are your subjects?'

'Physics, chemistry and biology.'

'Good God!'

'I hope He will be.'

'I took five O-levels and failed two. It's university and medicine after that, isn't it?'

'So they tell me.'

'You don't sound very keen.'

'You could be right.'

'Then why do it?'

'Good question. I think it's something to do with trying to do the right thing by people who think they are doing the right thing by you—if you see what I mean.'

Harold laughed. 'That's something I've never been very good at.'

'Anyway, I don't suppose it will work.'

Harold was standing in the little doorway at the foot of the spiral stone staircase, looking up. 'I haven't been up there since I was a kid.'

'Neither have I.'

'Shall we?'

'I expect it's pretty mucky, the pigeons have been roosting up there for years.'

Harold had climbed the first few steps. 'It doesn't look too bad. Coming?'

'If I must.'

The oak timbers and flooring were sound and above the ground floor window frames were intact with a good deal of glass still in place. Pigeons and bats had been in occupation but somebody had made an attempt to clean up. On the third floor they found a small brazier and a canvas bag containing coloured wooden wands, a sword, and other oddments which could have been theatrical 'props'.

Alice said, 'Laura?'

Harold looked embarrassed. 'I suppose so.'

'I didn't know she used this place.'

'Neither did I.'

Stout wooden steps led up to the trap-door which opened easily and they were out on the roof. It was heavily leaded and sloped gently from a central point to the battlements. On the grey, scaly lead someone had painted a pentagram in vermilion paint and the pentagram was almost but not completely enclosed in a double circle painted in the same manner.

Alice looked at Harold but said nothing.

On the side facing the estuary the view from the top of the tower was little different from that at the bottom, but on the landward side, being clear of the trees, they could see the house and grounds and the countryside for miles around; as far as St Agnes Beacon and Carn Brea and away to the mountainous white clay-tips near St Austell.

Alice said, 'I'd forgotten how nice it was up here; I wouldn't mind living in the tower.'

'You'd need a lift.'

'The stairs would be all right if they were cleaned up.'

Harold was standing in one of the embrasures, looking out over the estuary. Inky black rain clouds were gathering out to sea and in one place he could see the oblique smoky trail of a shower. He looked directly down, it seemed a very long way to the ground. The slate slab on which he was standing sloped slightly outwards as part of the watershed from the roof but his arms brushed the merlons on either side so there was little real danger of falling unless one played the fool. But his mother had fallen. Looking down again, he was for a moment almost overwhelmed by the thought of that breath-taking rush of air which had ended in a frightful, all-destroying thud.

'Harold, look!'

Alice was in the next embrasure but one and he joined her. She was pointing to an inscription freshly carved with great care and patience in the slate: Deborah Care 1963. Aged 26.

Alice said, 'That's been done recently.'

'Looks like it.'

'But who by?'

'Laura, I suppose.'

He said it defensively and Alice was embarrassed. 'I'm sorry, I'm being stupid. I just didn't realize she felt like that.' She looked at her watch, 'If we want any food it's time we were getting back. Coming?'

They went down the stone steps and down the path through the woods in silence. As they came out of the trees into the park, Alice said, 'I remember when I was five or six—you must have been about ten, you had a soprano voice and they made you sing your party piece for Christmas, O for the Wings of a Dove. You were all dolled up in a surplice and I thought you must be an angel.'

Harold brightened. 'You should hear me sing now.'

'Soprano?'

'*Do* you mind?' He slapped her bottom playfully and took her arm. 'Listen!' He started to sing the aria in a mellow tenor voice. 'Come on, join in!' They sang together, Alice's shaky contralto mingling with his tenor until they collapsed laughing.

Harold said, 'To think you've been around all this time and I haven't noticed!'

Alice said, 'Perhaps I'm going to like having you home. You make me feel human—almost.'

As they walked up to the house she caught him looking at the imposing frontage with an oddly intent expression. He was thinking, I'm trapped, well and truly. Is that what I really wanted?

'How does it feel—the young heir bit?'

'Oh, God, Alice, don't! It would be bad enough if there was any money but as things are ... Let's hope that father lives to be ninety-nine at least. Sometimes I wish that John and I could change places, he might enjoy skimping and slaving to replace a few tiles or put new lead in the valleys or whatever needs to be done.'

Alice said, 'Seriously, if you had a lot of money, from Aunt Lucille or from the pools, or anywhere, would you spend it on the estate?'

He answered diffidently, as though somewhat ashamed. 'I probably would. Daft, isn't it?'

'No, it's not daft, but why would you?'

He stopped at the bottom of the impressive granite steps. 'I don't know; I don't even like living here very much. My ego isn't on this scaie, it would fit better into a semi with two up and two down.'

Isobel said, 'I think I'll take Cleo for a run.'

The table had been cleared of the debris of lunch and Alice was helping her mother with the washing up.

Celia said, 'I suppose you know that it's raining.'

'Yes, but we are neither of us soluble.' Isobel went upstairs and came down wearing an old mackintosh of superior lineage and a waterproof hat. Cleo came out from under the table and joined her with no great show of enthusiasm.

When they were gone Celia said to Alice, 'Isobel is a very strange woman.'

By the time Isobel and Cleo entered the wood it was raining hard and Cleo kept to heel, head, ears and tail drooping. Isobel too, was depressed; she was in no doubt that Laura was baiting her. 'Bitch!' she muttered.

48

When they reached Tresean the french windows were closed and there was no sign of Payne. She had to go round to the door at the side of the house and ring. She could hear the piano; he was playing Schumann, the Abegg Variations, the only Schumann piece Isobel could be sure of recognizing. That should be a good mark. But she had to ring several times before he heard her and came to answer the door.

'Isobel! I wasn't expecting you. My goodness, you're wet!' He sounded less than enthusiastic. 'I'm in the sitting-room . . .'

He took her mackintosh and shook it outside before hanging it in the hall.

'I suppose Cleo will be happy here.' Which meant that he did not want wet dog in his sitting-room.

Already it was going wrong and she could have cried with vexation.

The sitting-room was at the back of the house and looked out on a walled garden, a rain-drenched wilderness. It was not a large room, just big enough for a baby-grand, a comfortable leather sofa and a couple of armchairs. Outside the sky was overcast and trees shut out a good deal of what light there was.

'I heard you playing Schumann.' Isobel tried to seed the conversation.

'Yes.'

'I had to come, Tim. I warned you about Laura, and last night at dinner . . .' She broke off as a new thought occurred to her. 'You didn't tell her about us?'

'Of course not!'

'Then she found out somehow. She announced, apropos of nothing, that you had a mistress—a *mistress*, even the word was aimed at me.'

He smiled. 'You think that the word, mistress, singles you out in some way?'

'You know exactly what I mean! It's a word nobody uses these days—it's dated, like me, and she used it to make sure that I got the message.'

They were still standing and Payne, with some irritation, said,

'Do sit down, Isobel. I'm sorry if you were embarrassed but I think you are making too much of it. Even if you are right we have done nothing which, as responsible adults, we are not free to do.'

She did not know what response she had expected or wanted but this was not it; there was no warmth in his manner, he was patronising her and this made her spiteful. 'She also said that you keep a revolver in a drawer of your desk.'

He frowned. 'Did she? I had no idea she knew about it. In any case I shall have to get rid of it.'

'I told you that it was a mistake to get mixed up with her, Tim; she's a trouble-maker.'

Isobel was sitting in one of the armchairs but he had remained standing. She sensed that he wanted to keep his distance. She thought, From the first time Laura's name was mentioned he began to see me as I am and now he no longer wants me.

His voice was matter-of-fact, detached, 'I haven't, as you put it, "got mixed up with her", Isobel. She comes here as I told you to consult my mother's books. I am quite prepared to believe that she might enjoy playing the *enfant terrible* but she can't possibly harm either you or me.'

She noticed that he had pointedly avoided saying 'us'. She had thought of him as meticulously kind, now it was clear that he could be cruel with the same virtuosity. She stood up.

'You are not going already?'

'I have to get back but I wanted you to know what had happened.'

'It's still raining; won't you at least wait until it stops?'

'I don't think there is much prospect of that and I have things to do.'

In the hall, while she was putting on her mackintosh, she said. 'Perhaps it will be better if I don't come here for a while.'

He expressed only mild surprise. 'Really? You take it that seriously?'

His unprotesting acceptance was like a slap in the face.

'Yes, I do.'

He stood under the canopy of the doorway and watched her as

she walked down the drive with Cleo following miserably at heel. She did not turn round.

'They hate me!'

Laura had repeated these words to herself so often and for so long that she could not remember when it all began, but in her thoughts she placed the beginning at the time of her mother's death. She told herself that from that very day she had been treated differently, that she had been excluded, driven in upon herself and her own resources.

'They hated my mother, now they hate me!'

She recalled incidents which had occurred when she was still only a little girl, occasions when she had been treated harshly or unjustly and she had whispered to herself, 'They hate me!' Over the years those words had acquired the soothing effect of a ritual response as when Celia murmured to herself, 'Holy Mary, mother of God . . .'

Sometimes she felt like a timid animal removed from its natural cover and exhibited; at others she was rebellious and filled with blind aggression. Surely Harold must have suffered in the same way? But he did not seem to mind; in fact he seemed to be unaware that the two of them had been singled out in this manner.

She had escaped, first to boarding school, then to her aunt in Paris, but it had not been a real escape for she had begun to ask herself, 'Why should they?' and later, 'Why should they get away with it?'

Her interest in the occult had come about because she saw in it another avenue of escape, escape into a world of blurred outlines and of vast and vague promise. But she had soon realized that with self discipline she might recapture more of that time before her mother's death, time which she now saw as if surrounded by a golden aura, and which hitherto she could recall only in tantalizing glimpses.

More recently still, in the darker rituals of magic, she thought she had seen the possibility of acquiring greater knowledge and greater authority and she had begun to tell herself, 'They deserve to be punished.'

She was in her room, seated in the lotus position before her little table. Outside, the rain had stopped but the sky remained overcast and the only indication that the sun was setting was an orange glow over the plantation, a glow which filled her room with a melancholy, golden light.

Laura was preparing herself for a first venture into ritual magic. She had gone without food for twenty-four hours, now she was spending time in contemplation in order to achieve serenity in both body and mind. She remained all but motionless while the light faded into darkness, then she got to her feet, stiffly at first, and went downstairs to the library to telephone. She dialled a number.

'Freda?' Freda was her partner at the shop. 'I think the weather is all right . . . Yes, but have you prepared yourself properly? . . . All right, I'll meet you at the drive gates in half-an-hour . . . No, I shall be walking; we'll use your car and leave it in the lane just below Piper's Cottage . . .'

Chapter Three

SUNDAY MORNING WAS the kind of June day one imagines in January, the air balmy and still, the sunlight limpid and gentle. Breakfast was over and Nancy had come upstairs to make the beds in the communicating rooms where she and Henry slept. She stood by the open window of her own room, looking across the park to the estuary. Though it was still short of ten o'clock boats with red and white sails were weaving about and a succession of small motor boats forged across her field of view—family parties bound, hopefully, for some secluded cove where there was sand for the children and safe bathing. She remembered such days from her childhood; coarse sand between the toes; lank hair, stiff with salt; sun-dried skin, deliciously warm and smooth as velvet. Mostly she remembered the promise of such mornings when it seemed that something rare and delectable was sure to happen before the day was out.

But this Sunday, like most summer Sundays, meant a busy day at the nursery when people came out from the town to buy a shrub or bedding plants, a bale of peat or a bag of fertilizer, or one of those horrid little plastic 'features'. It was good for business for Nancy to be there; customers liked to be served by Lady Care in person.

Ethel was dressing and titivating herself for morning service. Isobel would drive her to church in Henry's old Rover and they would sit in the family pew where Cares had sat for three hundred and fifty years. She liked to think that she was pointed out to strangers, 'That's old Lady Care.'

Isobel zipped up a blue knitted frock which was too tight for her and tried to decide between her gold chain with a cross and her white coral necklace. Her eyes met their reflection in the dressing-table mirror and she thought, You're fifty; what have you got to look forward to now? She felt the tears smarting in her eyes. Damn and blast that bloody girl!

Celia had been to early Mass and she was at the sink in the kitchen cleaning lettuce for lunch; the sun did not reach into the kitchen so it was chilly and, but for the ticking of the clock, quite silent. For an instant she saw herself utterly cut off from the world, adrift in that ugly, cold, damp kitchen for the rest of her life. She shivered. Alice came in wearing a thin cotton frock over her bikini.

'Can I help?'

'No.'

Alice picked up a half-slice of tinned pineapple from a dish on the table and popped it into her mouth.

'Alice!'

'Harold and I are going over to Lime Quay for a swim. We shall be back before lunch. Is that all right?'

'Harold?' Celia injected surprise and disapproval into her voice.

'Yes.'

'You've got your physics paper tomorrow, I thought you would want to do some last minute revision.'

Alice clenched her fists. 'Oh, mum! Can't you see I'm trying to forget the bloody exams for once?'

'There's no need to swear. What I say won't make any difference anyway, so why ask?'

Alice looked at her mother's back with a kind of despair. 'I'll be back before lunch. 'Bye!' She went out of the back door, slamming it behind her.

Celia muttered. 'Please God she passes her exams and please God she doesn't get herself mixed up with that boy. She's got brains. All she's got to do is to make the effort for a few years and she's *free*, free for life. Why is she so *blind*?'

Laura had not got to bed until nearly three and she had slept badly, disturbed by dreams that were prosaic enough but seemed to hint at nameless terrors. When she finally woke in broad daylight she looked at her watch and was astonished to see that it was ten o'clock. She had a dull headache which started at the base of her skull and reached over the top of her head to her eyes. She lay on her back, staring at the ceiling; she had a prickly feeling in her throat and her chest felt slightly congested. The smoke. Then she remembered Freda and her paroxysm of coughing. She felt angry. If only I had been alone . . .

At the climax of the ritual she really had experienced something quite new. It was a feeling of release which she could not put into words; it was as if her true self which had hitherto been constrained and repressed, had broken out of its prison, expanded and taken giant form, like a genie newly released from its bottle. And she could have believed that she had similar powers, that she really could command the spirit world. And then that stupid coughing . . .

Next time . . .

She got up and went to the bathroom; it was a warm morning and her skin felt moist. She sponged herself down with cold water and felt better. Back in her room she put on her brown linen dress and nothing else; she liked to feel the slightly abrasive caress of the material as she walked. She was in a strange mood, both predatory and playful; if she had been a cat she would have caught a mouse and played with it for a long time before making the kill.

In the kitchen Celia turned to look at her. 'Oh, it's you. What's the matter, have you been crying?'

'Crying? No, what makes you ask?'

'Your eyes are red.'

'I didn't sleep very well.' It was the smoke, smoke from the herbs she had burned in the ritual.

She made herself coffee and drank it black. Her headache was almost gone.

'Is Harold about?'

'He's gone swimming with Alice.' Celia got the only satisfaction she was likely to get from that fact.

Laura went out into the yard and through into the adjoining stable yard. It was like a brilliantly lit stage set with exaggerated colours, bluish shadows, grey and green lichens on the cobbles, and on the boundary wall pale red coping tiles which glowed in the sunshine. A steady tapping noise came from one of the loose boxes which John had converted to a workshop. The door was open and Laura went in. John was at his bench, facing the light from the door, working away at a small wooden panel which he was carving in a low relief.

Laura stood beside him, watching him work; the design had been carefully drawn in pencil and represented two dragon-flies among reeds with a frog in one corner.

'That looks interesting; is it for something special?'

The relationship between the two of them was an uneasy one. John was totally vulnerable to sarcasm or mockery and Laura was adept at both. John stopped work, gouge in hand.

'It's for Aunt Isobel. Next Friday is her birthday.'

'Is it? I'd forgotten. I shall have to think of something to give her.' Laura was picking up his tools and putting them down again in a way which irritated him. 'A book—that's the thing; a book by Barbara Cartland—don't you think that would be a good idea?'

John said, seriously, 'I don't think I've ever read any books by Barbara Cartland.'

Laura laughed, her hand on his arm. 'I thought that was where Aunt Isobel got all her plots.' John did not smile and Laura went on, 'You really are too good to be true, Johnny boy!' Her manner was at once patronising and flirtatious.

'I wish you wouldn't call me Johnny, Laura.'

'Why not, for heaven's sake?'

'Because it's not my name and I don't like it.'

John resumed work and Laura pottered, looking at things which were hanging on the walls or standing on shelves, wood carvings, pots and little terracotta animals.

'Now that Harold is home the three of us ought to see more of each other, don't you think?'

John said nothing and she went on, 'You don't like Harold much, do you?'

'I don't dislike him. I don't suppose I know him very well and in any case he's a lot older than me.'

'Are you jealous of him?'

'Jealous?' John stopped work again and looked at her with puzzled eyes.

'Because he gets Nanselow and not you.'

'Why should I be jealous about that? Nanselow is nothing to do with me.'

Laura threw up her hands and laughed. 'I love you, Johnny boy, especially when you're self-righteous.'

John went on with his carving in silence while Laura took down items from the shelves, examined them and put them back again.

'You really are clever at potting, John. Why don't you do more of it? If you did the animals of the zodiac or something like that I could sell them in the shop and you could make some money.'

John considered the question soberly. 'I don't get much spare time but it's mainly because I haven't got a kiln. They let me use the one at school sometimes but there isn't often room for things that haven't been made in class.'

One of the pieces on the shelves was covered with a cloth.

'What's under that?'

'It's a thing which hasn't been fired. Please don't touch it, it's only leather hard.'

But it was too late, Laura had removed the cloth and taken the piece into her hands. It was the head and shoulders of a young girl.

'Why, it's Alice!' She turned the head this way and that, examining it from all angles. 'Don't get worked up, Johnny, it's really quite hard. It's very good, too. You've got that way she holds her head and that sort of half-smile to perfection. That I-know-I'm-better-than-you-but-I-can't-help-it look.'

John was tense with repressed anger but he forced himself to be polite. 'I didn't want anyone to see it. I probably shan't be allowed to put it in the school kiln because it might fracture. I've hollowed it out but there's still a good thickness of clay in places.'

'But how did you do it? Did she sit for you?'

57

'Of course she didn't sit for me. She doesn't know anything about it.' He looked anxious. 'And I hope you won't tell her. I worked from a couple of photographs and when I wasn't sure of anything all I had to do was to look at her.' He turned back to his carving. 'It's not very good really, it's lifeless.'

Laura placed the head on the bench and continued to study it. 'I think it's very good indeed.' She looked at him with a quizzical expression. 'You're in love with Alice, aren't you?'

'Don't be silly!'

'Do you have it off with her?'

John flushed in embarrassment and anger, but said nothing.

'Dangerous waters, John.'

'I don't know what you're talking about.'

'Does she ever talk to you about her father?'

'Her father?'

'Yes, she must have had one, does she ever talk about him?'

'No.'

'Isn't that a bit odd?'

'I've never thought about it.'

'Doesn't it ever seem strange to you that nobody admits knowing anything about him? I mean, you can understand Celia being reticent, but the others, grandmother, Nancy, Aunt Isobel, father . . .'

John said stubbornly. 'It's nothing to do with me.'

'Perhaps not. But it surprises me that Alice isn't more interested in finding out about him. I'm sure she could if she wanted to and in similar circumstances, I should want to. But it's her affair.'

'Yes.'

Laura picked up the clay head, holding it between her hands so that she seemed to be studying its features. 'Have you ever read *Moll Flanders*, John?'

John was taken by surprise. 'Isn't it a book by the chap who wrote *Robinson Crusoe*?'

'Defoe, that's it. I wonder if Alice has ever read it. Life can be quite tricky if you don't know who you really are.' She reached up to return the head to its place on the shelf and as she did so it seemed to slip through her hands. It hit the floor with a dull thud, the clay shape collapsed and split.

Laura covered her face with her hands. 'God! I've broken it. John, whatever can I do or say?'

John's complexion, always sallow, turned even more pale. He stood rigid, the gouge in his hand. 'It doesn't matter.'

'It was a pure accident—you saw—'

John said quietly, 'Go away, Laura, I don't want you here.'

Alice stood on the edge of the quay, poised; she raised herself on her toes and dived, entering the water without too much splash. She surfaced, sweeping the hair from her eyes and gasping with the shock of the cold water.

'It's lovely!'

'Liar!'

Harold still hesitated but she had shamed him and he finally dived. 'God! It's cold.'

'Nonsense!'

They swam and he chased her; she allowed herself to be caught and pulled under by one foot. First steps in the choreographic routine which has changed little since Adam and Eve bathed in some backwater of the Euphrates—or was it the Tigris? At this stage the routine is completed by treading water, arms linked, and a wet kiss.

'Race you back to the steps.'

She won by several lengths.

'You swim well.'

'I've had more practice than you.'

'Says she, modestly.'

They dived, swam again, and played infantile games as a cover for mild sexual advances then they sat on the edge of the quay, legs dangling, to dry in the sun.

'Did anyone ever tell you that you are good to look at?'

'No.'

'Then what sort of boys have you been going out with?'

'None.'

'I don't believe that.'

'Suit yourself, but it's time we were moving.'

As they were walking back along the length of the quay they saw Henry trudging homeward with his easel and canvas.

As was sometimes the case on Sundays the party in the kitchen was at full strength with standing room only for some. Ethel worked away at a plate of ham and salad; she looked across at Alice.

'What have you done with your hair?'

'I've been swimming, I shall have to wash it.'

'In my day we wore bathing hats. Come to think of it we wore other things as well, now you go naked.'

'Not quite, gran.'

'As good as.'

Henry was lolling against the sink, holding a plate of salad which he scooped into his mouth with a fork. His jaws worked with the regular rhythm of a machine. 'Your exams start tomorrow, don't they? What is it?'

'Physics tomorrow.'

Henry bit into a tomato and grinned. 'Believe it or not, Alice, I used to do physics at school. In my day it was all about weightless scale-pans attached to cords which ran over frictionless pulleys.'

Alice grinned back. 'Sounds like fun.'

'Of course, that was only O-level or School Certificate as they called it then.'

Celia thought, What children men are when it comes to sex. More than thirty years younger, she could twist him round her little finger any time she wanted to. Age is defeat for a woman.

Harold was standing near his sister and watching Alice. Ethel added a slice of ham to some salad on a plate and passed it to him. 'Here, eat that, boy, or you'll go like your sister.'

Cleo sprawled on the stone floor under the table gnawing at a mutton bone which she held between her paws. Laura sat on a stool by the range, nibbling a water-biscuit which she occasionally dipped into a tub of cottage cheese. She was watching Harold through her glasses.

'Where did you get to this morning? I was looking for you.'

Despite himself, Harold flushed. 'I went swimming with Alice; did you want me for something?'

'Nothing important. I had an interesting time with John in his workshop. I had no idea of the clever things he's taught himself to do.'

John did not raise his eyes from his plate.

Celia got up from her place at the table, collected her knife, fork and plate and took them over to the sink where Henry was standing. Laura saw them exchange glances; a message had passed; a message so familiar through repetition that a meeting of the eyes for a fraction of a second was a sufficient signal.

Before most of the others had finished Laura took herself off. Although she was farthest from the door and had to make her way past the others it was some time before they noticed that she had gone.

'That girl can make herself invisible.'

'That's how she finds out things.'

In her room Laura changed her brown linen dress for a sophisticated blue silk frock, very simple and very expensive, which her aunt had bought her in Paris. She studied the result in the mirror then brushed her hair until it shone like the proverbial gold. She spent some time trying to decide whether to catch it back with a jewelled slide but finally rejected the slide in favour of a length of blue riband used as a bandeau. It was unusual for her to take such trouble with her appearance.

When she was ready she went downstairs and let herself out by the side door. To avoid the muddy paths through the woods she went by way of the drive. At the gates she turned down Ferry Road then off the road, along a lane between high hedges which led to Tresean. It was hot and still and silent. She walked up the drive under the beech trees and crossed the grass. The french windows were open but the room was empty.

'Tim!'

There was no response so she crossed the room and went through into the hall. After the brilliance of the sunshine outside she had difficulty in seeing. She called again but there was still no answer. She opened a door on the opposite side of the hall and entered a pleasant room with a grand piano and a large window overlooking a neglected garden. Someone was lounging in an old steamer chair in the garden; she could see one arm trailing and a book on the grass. There was a door into the garden and she opened it quietly; she crept across the grass and stood looking down at Payne who was fast asleep, his mouth slightly open. She picked a flowering grass stalk and tickled his nose.

Payne opened his eyes, startled, but recovered quickly. 'I'm dreaming.'

'You think so? Shut your eyes and try again.'

He did so. 'It's a very persistent dream and I like it. Am I allowed to say that you look lovely?'

'Thank you.'

He stood up. 'Would you prefer to go inside or shall we stay out here?'

'Out here, please.' Laura was smiling, gentle, agreeable.

'I'll get another chair.' He stopped on his way to the house. 'A drink?'

'I don't take alcohol.'

'I know. Tea, coffee, or mineral water?'

'What does Isobel have?'

He gave a wry smile. 'Tea.'

'Then I'll have mineral water.'

He came back with another deck chair and a tray with mineral water and ice cubes. 'Is that to madam's satisfaction?'

'Entirely.'

They sat side by side, Laura with her bare legs stretched out to the sun.

Payne said, 'I gather that you've been very naughty.'

'Oh? Tell me.'

'I think you know already. Apparently you announced to your assembled family that I have a mistress.'

Laura chuckled like a mischievous schoolgirl caught out. 'I wanted to see Isobel blush—and she did, but I didn't give her away.'

Payne was watching her with curiosity. 'Why did you tell them I had a gun?'

She turned to him as though surprised. 'Did Isobel say I told them that?'

'Yes.'

She frowned. 'How odd!'

'Why do you find it odd?'

'Well, I don't suppose it matters who said it but, in fact, it was Isobel herself. How would I know whether you had a gun or not?'

'How extraordinary!'

'I suppose one should feel sorry for her but she's been behaving very strangely recently. It must be her menopause. Incidentally, do you have a gun, or did she make it up?'

'No, it's quite true. I do have an old service revolver which belonged to my father. He was an army man.'

'I see.'

It was hot, so hot that the birds were silenced. The garden was several years on its way back to nature; young trees, saplings, old shrubs, waist-high grass and patches of nettles—a paradise for butterflies. The only clear patch was where they were sitting, near the house.

'Don't you like gardening?'

'I prefer the way nature does it.'

'What a clever excuse for being lazy!' She settled back in her chair and put her hands behind her head. 'It's lovely here—relaxing.'

He made no attempt to disguise the fact that he was watching her every movement. They were silent for a long time; her eyes were closed and he began to wonder if she was asleep then, abruptly, she said, 'You've been here since I was eleven or twelve years old and we've only just really met.'

'Yes.'

'You've lived here all that time on your own?'

'Yes.'

'What did you do before you came here?'

'I was a lecturer at a university in the north.'

'Why did you stop being a lecturer?'

'Because I was not greatly in need of the money and there were other things I wanted to do. I wanted, as they say in these days, to do my own thing.'

'The philosophers of the Romantic Movement.'

'Yes.'

'Have you been married?'

'Yes.'

'Children?'

'No.'

'Did the break with your wife come at the same time as your break with the job?'

'You are very perceptive.'

'And very inquisitive. But we are friends, aren't we?'

'I hope so, very much.'

'You can't have lived all those years like a monk.'

'No, I don't think I should do very well as a monk. I go away from time to time.'

He reached out his hand and rested it on her thigh. 'Do you mind?'

'I'll tell you when I do.'

Very gently he kneaded the muscles of her inner thigh.

'I suppose you want to go to bed with me?'

'You are very direct.' He laughed nervously. 'But the answer, as they say, is in the affirmative—which means, yes.'

She started to laugh.

'Why are you laughing?'

'I wondered if I should say, "Another time, perhaps."'

He laughed with her. 'You are a strange girl.'

'Woman—don't make any mistake about that.'

'You make yourself sound hard yet I know that there must be another side.'

'How do you know?'

'Because of your interest in the occult. Really hard people lack imagination and no one lacking in imagination could cope with Eliphas Levi.'

64

'I see.'

She was holding up her hands, shielding her face from the sun and they were so slender and delicate that the light seemed to pass through them. Payne watched her, his slightly bulging eyes speculative, wondering.

'Half witch, half angel; half seeress . . .' He stopped.

She said, 'You are a coward. Why don't you finish it? ". . . half seeress, half liar; half child, half actress; half adventuress, half nun; half sleepwalker, half coquette."'

'So you know the quotation.'

'Since I've known you I've done my homework. I always do my homework.'

'There's a picture in my workroom of Bettina, reproduced from an engraving by Grimm. Something about her reminds me of you.'

'I've seen it. She's not in the least like me; she was a fat fraulein.'

'Not fat, just pleasantly plump.'

'I hate plump women!' She stood up abruptly. 'It's too hot here, let's go indoors.'

He followed her into the drawing room and they sat on the sofa with the door open to the garden.

'Am I allowed to ask about you?'

'What do you want to know?'

'You are twenty-one? Twenty-two?'

'Twenty-two.'

'The age at which Bettina seduced the fifty-eight year old Goethe.'

'You are not Goethe and I am not Bettina.'

'Neither am I fifty-eight years old.' He paused, smiling uncertainly. He could not make up his mind how to cope with Laura; she did not respond predictably. 'Do you have any boy—sorry, men friends?'

'None.'

'Is it to be marriage at some future time?'

'No.'

'That sounds final.'

'It is. At some time I may have a child but I have no intention of getting married. Marriage is a man's thing; keeping a woman for his private use.'

'Surely it works both ways?'

Laura sounded bored. 'Does it? You must explain to me some-time.'

'If you decide to have a baby you will need a man.'

'So they tell me; virgin birth seems to be a divine prerogative, more's the pity.'

'I wouldn't have thought that you were anti-sex.'

'I'm not in the least anti-sex; it's just that I would prefer my child to be mine and not half somebody else's.'

'A carbon copy?' His smile was back, he felt more sure of his ground. 'The biologists call it cloning.'

'Do they?' She was not interested. 'Is there anything wrong with wanting one's child to be like oneself?'

Payne's cat came in from the garden and looked with calculation at the arm of the sofa then, with a clean leap, landed neatly, crouched down, tucked in feet and tail, and was asleep.

Laura said, 'If I am to be reincarnated I hope it will be as a cat. Cats are satisfied with themselves and not in the least interested in what others think of them.'

Payne laughed.

Laura looked round the room with studied interest. 'This is a charming house; will you show me the rest of it sometime?'

'Now, if you wish.'

She followed him into the hall and up the dimly lit stairs with their carved and fretted banisters. He opened the door of his bedroom. She was dazzled by the small square of sunlight in the recessed window and it was a moment before she could make out the bed with its monstrously carved ends, the massive wardrobe and the fretted beams. The room had a slightly musty smell which was not unpleasant.

'It's like living inside a cuckoo clock, I feel I want to put my head out of the window and say, "Cuckoo!"'

She looked at the bed which was covered with a patchwork quilt. 'Is this where you and Isobel amuse yourselves?'

Payne did not answer. Laura took hold of the bedclothes and turned down the bed. She looked up at the beams and the high, wooden ceiling. 'There must be spiders up there.'

'They only come out at night.'

'I hope so.' She stood with her back to him. 'You can unzip me.'

She stepped out of the blue silk dress and laid it across the foot of the bed; she wore no slip and no brassière, only panties.

'Aren't you going to undress?' She pulled the bedclothes right back and lay on the bed. 'Do you have Isobel naked?'

Payne was unbuttoning his shirt. She looked impossibly slender and fragile, too perfect to be real, a child-woman with slim straight limbs and scarcely nubile breasts, but a fine line of golden hairs started below her navel and vanished into her panties. Payne got on the bed at her side, still wearing his Y-fronts. He supported himself on one elbow and with his free hand smoothed the hair from her forehead and kissed the tip of her nose. His hand moved to her breasts which he fondled with practised skill.

'I'm probably too thin for you—especially after Isobel; that must be like making love to sponge rubber.'

'Let's forget about Isobel.'

'If you like. Aren't you going to take my pants off?'

Payne slid his hand down inside her panties and she arched her back to make it easier for him.

'Now yours . . . Your hair is going white down there.'

He tried to hide his embarrassment with forced humour. 'I'm an old man—do you mind?' He stroked her thighs.

'Have you had many women?'

'I would rather not think about other women. I only want to think about one woman—you.'

'But what if I want to talk about your other women? It might excite me—turn me on. Isn't that what you're trying to do?'

'All right, I have had other women but none so . . .' He searched for the exact word as a matter of habit. 'None so exquisite as you. That is the simple truth.' With the tip of one finger he traced delicate patterns in her silky pubic hair.

67

She was lying on her back, legs together, arms at her side, totally unresponsive. 'I'm not a virgin.'

'No?' He smiled. 'I didn't think that you were.'

'How do you feel when you take a girl's virginity. Does it give you a thrill to take away something she can never regain?'

Irritation betrayed itself in his voice. 'I've not had much experience but, in any case, a man does not *take* a girl's virginity unless he rapes her; it is offered, as a gift.'

Laura gave one of her rare laughs. 'How very nice! The perfect gentleman, even in bed. Was that what happened with the girls at your university?'

Payne's hand was suddenly still. 'I don't know what you are talking about.'

'Your students—as I heard it you made a habit of taking your girl students to bed. Perhaps they weren't all virgins. What about the one who killed herself—was she?'

Payne got off the bed and stooped to pick up his underpants. 'You've been listening to gossip.'

Laura did not move. 'No, I've been doing my homework; I warned you that I always do. It doesn't make me think any the less of you. If the girl was fool enough to kill herself that was her affair, wasn't it?'

Payne was buttoning his shirt, fumbling with buttons.

Laura rolled on her side to watch him. 'You can still have me if you want me.'

Payne said, 'Isobel warned me about you.'

'You should have listened. Aunt Isobel knows best. Did you know that she does a column for a teenagers' magazine? Advising the lecherous little beasts on how to conduct their love lives. Can you imagine?'

Payne was zipping up his trousers. 'I shall be downstairs.'

Laura got off the bed and dressed; she spent a little while doing her hair. Finally she went downstairs. Payne came to the door of the drawing room.

'I'm sorry. You had a perfect right to make enquiries about me, but to set the record straight you should know that the girl who killed herself did not even tell me that she was pregnant. If she had—'

'If she had, you would have arranged a nice, tidy, hygienic, safe abortion.'

Payne said, primly, 'I would have helped her.'

'Was she the reason you left university?'

He nodded. 'Yes, the university authorities take a poor view of that sort of thing and you can't really blame them.'

'Your wife too?'

'My wife too.'

'Good!'

'What's good about it?'

'It's good that I'm finding out about you.'

'Does that mean that I shall see you again?'

'If you want to. Now let's change the subject. Last night I tried a ritual summoning.'

'You did? Did it work?'

They went into the drawing room again and sat on the settee.

'No, it didn't work, I made the mistake of using Freda as my assistant.'

'Freda?'

'My partner at the shop.' Laura shifted her position, tucking her legs under her. 'She got smoke from the brazier down her lungs and at the crucial moment she went off into a fit of coughing. I could have killed her.'

'Where did all this happen?'

'At the top of the Prospect Tower.'

'Good God! You're really serious about this, aren't you?'

'I'm serious about most things.'

'Shall you try again?'

'Yes, but not with Freda.'

John went into the library where Isobel was working at her table by the window.

'No homework at half-term, surely, John?'

'No, Aunt Isobel, I just want to look something up.'

Many of the more valuable books from the library had been sold long ago and there were great gaps on the shelves but there remained a tolerable collection of reference books though most of them were out of date. He found an old *Oxford Companion* and turned to the entry for *Moll Flanders*. He read the synopsis and at first it had no special significance for him then a single phrase stood out as though it had been printed in bolder type: '*and discovers that she had unwittingly married her own brother.*'

Laura had been making insinuations about Alice's parents. He had not wanted to listen. He did not need to be told that people sometimes behaved in discreditable ways but he preferred to think of his family with affection and respect—really, to take them for granted and get on with his own life. It was the future that mattered, not what people had done in the past. But this was different; it mattered a very great deal. He closed the book and put it back on the shelf.

'Did you find what you wanted?'

'Yes, thank you, Aunt Isobel.'

Isobel looked at him more closely. 'Are you all right, John? You look upset.'

He put on a forced smile. 'Nothing wrong with me, Aunt Isobel. I'm fine.'

Isobel glanced round at the empty shelves. 'It's sad, isn't it? When I was young, this was a real library.'

'Yes . . . Yes, I expect it was.'

Laura had said, 'You're in love with her, aren't you?' He had told her not to be silly and she had smiled and said, 'Deep waters, John.'

John clenched his teeth. 'Laura!'

He knew that what Laura had suggested could possibly be true but he could not believe it—not his father . . . My father and Aunt Celia—he called her aunt though she was some sort of cousin. Father and Alice's mother—he tried thinking about it in different ways and none was credible. It just could not be, it must not be! But *if* . . . If it was true had Alice any idea of it? He clenched his fists and wished that his life could be his own; a clean sheet on which nobody would write but himself.

At seven o'clock he joined the others in the old breakfast room for the evening meal. Nine of them sat round the refectory table which was so worn that the grain stood up in ridges. Three generations. Whatever anybody said or thought they were still a family, a family living in the family home. That mattered too.

His mother was serving soup from the big tureen which he remembered from infancy. It was blue and white with a picture of Warwick Castle on the lid. Once there had been a whole dinner service to match, now all that remained was the tureen and a few plates. Bowls of hot soup were being passed from hand to hand.

'What is it tonight, Celia?' Granny liked her food.

'Lentil.'

'With orange and coriander?'

'Taste it and see.'

His father was talking to Laura who listened with unusual attention.

'It occurred to me after you were talking about that gun of Payne's; his father was an officer in the East Lancs . . . I remember Payne telling me when he first came to Tresean . . .'

John tried to see his father as a stranger might see him; the thin sandy hair, the wispy little beard, the pink cheeks like rosy apples, the candid blue eyes . . . He was a messy eater, already his moustache and beard were stained with the orange soup. John loved him for all these things but surely he must strike people as . . . as eccentric, even a little comic? Not the sort to . . . But John had to admit to himself that he had not the slightest idea what special sort of man was likely to have affairs with women.

His father and Laura were still talking about Payne.

Laura was saying, 'Did you find out much about him when he came here?'

'The agent took up the usual references.'

Laura sipped soup from her spoon with the delicacy of an insect sipping nectar, and quite illogically John hated her for it. 'I meant, did you find out what it was that made him pack up whatever it

71

was he was doing and hide himself away down here?'

Henry wiped his mouth with his napkin. 'Oh, that! I know that he was teaching at one of the northern universities—I forget which. I don't think he liked it much; he didn't get enough time for his own research. Anyway, he didn't have to earn his living; his mother was a Haskin and when she died he inherited a large block of shares in Haskin's Electrical Supplies. Lucky man!'

Laura said, 'So, as far as you know, there was no scandal?'

Henry looked surprised. 'Scandal? No, certainly not—nothing like that with Payne, he's not the sort.'

His Aunt Isobel was stirring her soup as if to cool it though it was already on the cold side. In fact it was obvious even to John that she was following Laura's conversation with her father, and too preoccupied to think of food.

John felt frustrated. He could not begin to grasp what went on between the members of his own family. Growing up was like being precipitated into the middle of a complicated television play and trying to sort out the characters and their relationships. Surely it was not like that in all families?

He tried not to look at Alice who was sitting opposite him, next to Harold, but his eyes kept coming back to her. She was wearing a red dress which seemed to shimmer in the dim light. She and Harold exchanged remarks from time to time—just short sentences, inaudible across the table, but giving an unmistakable impression of intimacy. Her face was unusually animated and he felt a pang of intense jealousy.

He thought, If father is . . . but he drove the very idea from his mind.

'You're very quiet tonight, John. Is it school tomorrow that's upsetting you?' It was his grandmother, sitting next to him.

'What? No, gran, I'm not upset, I was just thinking.'

'Then perhaps you would think about passing me the bread.'

'Sorry!'

John tapped on the door of Alice's room. He thought he heard her answer and opened the door. She had been lying on the bed revising and she had raised herself on one elbow to see who it was. He felt sure that she was disappointed.

'Hullo, what do you want?'

It was late evening and the little room at the back of the house seemed depressingly dark.

'Shall I switch on the light?'

'If you like.'

He wanted the atmosphere to be less sombre but the yellow light seemed to make the little room even more depressing.

'Did you want something?' Alice sat up, drawing her feet under her.

John pretended to look at the books on the shelves. 'I wanted to talk to you about something.'

'Well, you're talking to me; get on with it, John.'

'I was in my workshop this morning and Laura came in. After a bit she started to talk about your father . . .'

'*My* father.' Alice's voice sounded suddenly hard.

'Yes, she said it was funny nobody seemed to know who he was.'

Alice swung her legs off the bed and sat on the edge, looking up at him. 'Is it any business of Laura's or of yours?'

John flushed. 'Don't get angry with me, Alice; this is very difficult.'

'All right, go on.'

'Then she asked me if I had ever read *Moll Flanders* . . .' He broke off and looked at the girl, hoping that he might not have to say any more but Alice's expression was blank. 'I told her I hadn't.'

'Well?'

'It's a book by Daniel Defoe.'

'I know it's a book by Defoe; I saw it as a serial on TV. What about it?'

'Then Laura said, "I wonder if Alice has ever read it . . ."'

Alice stood up abruptly and walked over to the window. 'Are you going to tell me what all this is about or are we playing some sort of guessing game?'

'I looked up the book in the *Oxford Companion* where it summarized the story; it's about a girl who without knowing it . . .'

Alice's expression changed and she said in a low voice, 'A girl who without knowing it married her brother.' She laughed briefly in a way that worried him. 'I was being stupid; I might have known with Laura.'

John blundered on, 'It's very important to me—'

She turned on him. 'Important to you! Why the hell should it matter to you?' Then she saw his face and her manner softened. She reached out and held his arm. 'I'm sorry, John, I didn't mean to snap at you.'

'It's all right.'

Alice said, 'You know what Laura is trying to do, don't you?'

'I think so, but if it's not true . . .'

Her anger flared once more, 'How do I know whether it's true or not?'

That night Henry joined Nancy in her bed. She smiled at him as he came in, comically diffident, and put down the book she was reading.

'Lonely?'

'You could say that.'

She pushed back the bedclothes and made room for him by her side. When they were lying together she said, 'Have you seen John this evening?'

'Not since dinner. Why?'

'He's upset about something; I noticed it at lunch time and again at dinner. He hardly said a word.'

'I expect he's got something on his mind.'

'Of course he's got something on his mind—that's what I'm telling you, but what?'

'I've no idea.'

Nancy said, 'John isn't easily upset; I don't like to see him like that. I wonder if he is jealous of Harold?'

'Why should he be?'

'Because Alice is spending time with Harold which she used to spend with him.'

Henry laughed. 'Women are always looking for trouble. The four of them are just like brothers and sisters; they've been brought up together. Harold's been away a long time and it's natural Alice should want to spend a bit more time with him. If John is upset about that . . .'

Henry bent over his wife and kissed her on the lips. 'I've got a problem of my own to settle so let's start by getting this damned nightgown off . . .'

Chapter Four

ON TUESDAY ISOBEL, Celia, Harold and Laura were all in the kitchen at lunch time. Alice had been sitting her first chemistry paper and was due back at any moment. Laura had come home, leaving her partner in the shop as she sometimes did when business was slack.

Isobel said, 'How are you getting on in your new job, Harold?'

Harold was self-conscious about his work in the estate office. 'All right, I think, Aunt Isobel.'

'What are they giving you to do?'

'Well, so far I've been sorting out the estate maps and making a catalogue but this afternoon Captain Holiday is going in to town to see Wickett, the lawyer, and I am to go with him.'

The work of the estate office had always been surrounded by a certain mystique, penetrated only by Henry himself. As children they had been forbidden to play in the area round the stable block for fear of disturbing the captain and his assistant and so they had grown up with an almost religious respect for the rites which were performed in that gloomy office.

Celia said, 'Does this mean that you are home for good?'

'I don't know; father said he wanted me to get to know the ropes.'

Celia sniffed. 'Well, it's certainly time somebody did.'

The sun was high enough to shine into the yard and the kitchen door stood open. There were footsteps on the cobbles and Celia was immediately alert, expecting Alice, but it was Henry who came in.

'Somebody's been shooting in East Wood again; I picked up

several shells. It must be Dippy Saunders. I don't mind anybody taking pot-shots at the pigeons but that lout will loose off at anything that moves. I shall speak to his father; after all, it is my land.'

Nobody said anything and Henry made a sandwich for himself with two halves of a bread roll and a slice of cheese.

Laura was eating lettuce leaves and low-fat cottage cheese. She said to Celia, 'I shan't be in for a meal this evening. We are having a meeting.' A meeting of the *Society for Occult and Psychical Studies* which met in a room behind Laura's shop.

Celia ignored her, listening for Alice. 'I hope she managed that paper all right; she admitted that she would need luck with the questions. I knew she wasn't doing enough revision.'

Henry laughed, spluttering crumbs all over the place. 'Everybody needs luck with exam questions, Celia! You worry too much.'

'And you don't worry enough.' She glanced up at the yellow face of the clock. 'Half-past one. She ought to be here, the bus gets in at one and it's only twenty minutes' walk.' She added after a moment, 'She does it deliberately because she knows how anxious I am.'

Alice walked in while her mother was still speaking.

'Well?'

'Well what, mother?'

'Don't be aggravating, Alice! How did you get on with the chemistry?'

'It was all right, I suppose.'

'Did you do all the questions?'

'No, we were only supposed to do five.'

'Alice! You know exactly what I mean. Did you do all the questions you were supposed to do?'

Isobel cut in, 'For God's sake leave the girl alone, Celia! She's done her best, what's the good of holding an inquest?'

Harold pulled up a chair for Alice. 'Have some ham, it's very good.' He found a clean plate and put a slice of ham on it with some tomato and lettuce. Do you want some dressing?'

'No, thanks.'

77

Celia watched in silence. Laura's glasses were catching the light and it was impossible to say in exactly what direction she was looking.

Henry said, 'What is it tomorrow, Alice? Or shouldn't I ask?'

'Nothing in the morning, first biology in the afternoon.'

Celia got up to take dirty dishes to the sink and Laura turned, watching her every move. Then Laura said, 'I'm going up to my room,' and she got up and went out.

Almost immediately Alice pushed back her plate and followed her.

Celia turned to Harold, 'What is all that about?'

Harold looked blank, 'I've no idea.'

Henry said, 'I thought Alice looked a bit washed out, I suppose it's the exams.'

Later, Harold went upstairs to change into something more formal for his visit to the lawyer. He was naked, looking for a clean shirt, when Laura came in. He hated to be caught undressed by his sister and once he had complained about her habit of coming in without knocking but she had so ridiculed him that he hadn't the courage to persist.

She stood just inside the door. 'Going out?'

'I said downstairs that I was going with Captain Holiday to see the lawyer.' Harold was on the defensive.

'Did you? I didn't notice. I thought you would be going out with Alice as she's got a free afternoon.'

He tried to sound flippant. 'I'm a working man—remember?'

Laura came into the room and sat, straight-backed, on the edge of his bed. 'You seem to be getting on very well with Alice since you've been home this time.'

'I suppose I am. Before, what with school and that business course and the job, I scarcely knew her. In any case she was only a kid.'

'And now she's the right shape in all the right places so you go sniffing around her like a dog after a bitch on heat. Men are disgusting!'

Harold said nothing.

'Harold . . .'

'Yes? He was pulling on his shirt with his back to her.

'Don't you think we should try to find out the truth about how mother died?'

Harold was standing by the bed now, looking down at her. 'But we know how she died.'

'Do we?'

'She fell from the Prospect Tower.'

'Fell?'

Harold frowned. 'You think she might have killed herself; perhaps she did, but what satisfaction should we get from knowing it—even if it was possible to find out.'

Laura said, 'I've looked up the report of the inquest. Father said, in evidence, that she was in a very excitable state that afternoon. It was she who wanted to go up the tower—she said that she had never been to the top and she wanted to see the view. Anyway, when she got up there she went to stand in one of the embrasures and started to fool about—this is father's story—then she slipped and fell.'

'It could have happened like that—easily.'

'But what if she was pushed?'

'*Pushed*?' Harold looked at his sister in amazement. 'But that would make father a murderer! Really, Laura, that is a terrible thing to say; you've absolutely no reason—' Harold broke off. 'In any case, you told me that Nancy was with them.'

'She was.'

'Well, then . . .'

'She gave evidence at the inquest which agreed with father's.'

'In that case I really don't see what you are trying to say.'

'A few months later she was Lady Care.'

Harold was deeply shocked and it was a moment or two before he could find words. When he spoke at last his voice was uncertain and husky. 'What are you trying to do to us, Laura? Do you want to destroy us as a family, or what?'

'I want to know the truth about father and mother, about father and Nancy, about Celia and Alice—and about Isobel too, because you can depend on it that whatever went on, she knows about it.'

'But you haven't the slightest evidence that anything "went on".' He was excited and had difficulty in finding words. 'You brood too much on the past, Laura, you are becoming obsessed by it.'

It was the first time he had criticized his sister directly since they were children and it gave him a strange sense of recklessness.

'Even if what you say could possibly have happened—and I don't believe for a moment that it could—there would be no way of finding out.'

'I think that there might be.'

'How?'

'I will tell you when you are in a more receptive mood.'

Harold felt helpless and depressed; he had no illusions about his ability to influence Laura but he felt driven to try. 'You are making father out to be some sort of monster.'

'Not a monster; just a selfish and rather stupid man with a weakness for younger women.'

Harold did not know what to say or do.

Laura went on, 'When I was in Paris with Aunt Lucille I read all the letters mother had written to her.'

'Well?'

'Mother used to write to her every week and in several of her letters, especially towards the end, she said things like, "I drive Henry into such fits of desperation that one day I think he must kill me." Another time she wrote, "Sometimes I am afraid of Henry and I wonder what he will do . . ." Only a week before she died her letter ended, "I feel attracted to the idea of dying for I can think of nothing to live for and death could, just possibly, be the beginning of a new and more interesting adventure. So if Henry finally decides that he can stand me no longer, it might not be a bad thing for I should never screw up enough courage to take my own life."'

Harold regarded his sister with astonishment. 'You know those passages by heart.'

'They came from mother's heart.'

'Did you ask Aunt Lucille about them?'

'No, I wasn't supposed to see the letters. In any case, Aunt Lucille is on his side. In her eyes he can do very little wrong. She told me herself that if mother hadn't married him she would have done.' Laura smiled, 'Father exercises charm over a certain type of woman—or haven't you noticed?'

Laura climbed the path through East Wood, skirting the summit of the hill where the tower was and came to a point where she could look down on the lane and on Piper's Cottage. The roof of Tresean with its ornamental ridge-tiles was just visible through the trees away to her left, and to her right she could glimpse the river and the chain ferry which was on the opposite bank waiting for its quota of cars and people.

She pushed her way through a belt of thin scrub and came to a little clearing where she sat on a fallen tree and composed herself to wait. She was not in the least impatient but content to sit there in silence with her thoughts. A grey squirrel came down from a nearby tree and loped off about its business; brown butterflies fluttered weakly in and out of the shade and a large ground beetle investigated the toe of her shoe with its antennae. The ferry clanked across and was lost to her view.

She heard light footsteps on the path and a moment later, through the screen of leaves, she saw Alice. Alice walked along the path to the point where it dipped suddenly down the slope, and stood there, looking down into the valley.

They both waited and it was some minutes before they saw Celia coming down the lane towards the cottage. She wore slacks and a floral blouse and she carried a shopping bag. She stopped at the gate of the cottage, looked about her, then pushed open the gate and went up the steps to the front door. She must have had the key ready in her hand for there was scarcely a pause before she was inside and the door had closed behind her.

Another three or four minutes and Laura's father came into view. He walked with a certain swagger, striving to look natural and unconcerned. He too, went up the steps and into the cottage.

The cottage was ready for its first tenants, due in a few days.

Nancy had equipped the place down to the last detail in the belief that people are ready to pay high prices if the accommodation is right. The windows were small and the chintz curtains were drawn so that the interior seemed very dimly lit after the sunshine outside but the furniture and the paintwork gleamed and the whole place smelled of polish.

Celia went up the steep narrow stairs to the smaller of the two front bedrooms and drew back the curtains, flooding the little room with sunshine. The divan bed was not made up but she fetched a blanket from a chest on the landing and took a sheet from her shopping bag. She heard the gate open and looked out of the window. It was Henry. She heard him fumbling with the catch of the front door, then his footsteps on the stairs. He came in with a half-smile, like a child unsure of his welcome.

'Ah, there you are!'

Almost at once he started to undress her and said, as he always did, 'I like to undress my women.' He said it humorously but Celia knew that it conjured up for him dream pictures of a dozen lissom girls waiting on his slightest whim. She thought, Why do I put up with it? and she said, 'Why do I put up with you?'

He kissed her neck. 'Because you need me, as I need you.'

It was true, up to a point. She did not need sex particularly but she needed human contact. I need to be needed, she told herself. It was her justification, it helped her to come to terms with her Catholic conscience.

She was naked to the waist and Henry was kissing her breasts. In her clothes Celia looked lean, even a little stringy, but naked she displayed a surprising fullness and her skin had a pleasant lightly tanned look so that her nakedness was not blatant but seemed natural and becoming.

Henry said, 'You know, Celia, clothes don't do you justice.'

'No? That's comforting to know when I have to spend most of my life wearing them.'

Henry unzipped her slacks and rolled them down.

'You treat me like a paid whore.'

'Celia! That's not fair.'

Celia allowed herself to be laid on the bed while he dealt with her sandals, her slacks and her pants and she thought, What does he know or care about fairness now?

Henry undressed, adjusted the mirror of the dressing-table so that they could see themselves in bed, then lay down beside her. The hairs on his body were turning grey and this made Celia feel sad. It was all over fairly quickly and Henry rolled off her.

'I'm not what I was, Celia.'

'No?' She refused to bolster his ego; she had done enough.

They lay for a few minutes in the sunshine then Celia said, 'This has to stop, Henry.'

'Why?'

'Do I have to give you reasons? There are plenty, can't you think of them for yourself? The cottage is going to be let; I wouldn't have Alice find out about us for anything in the world; I'm in a state of mortal sin . . . Do you need any more?'

Henry smoothed the hair back from her forehead. 'We can find somewhere else and why should Alice ever get to know? As to the other, you go to confession, don't you?'

'I haven't been for a long time; I daren't. Going to confession isn't like buying a tin of baked beans in a supermarket, it's part of the sacrament of penance.'

'But you get absolution.'

Celia sighed. 'There must be a firm purpose of amendment, otherwise confession becomes a mockery.'

Henry shifted his hand to her breast, 'I need you, Celia.'

'And you are married to Nancy.'

'You know that I need more than one woman; I can't help it. I shall end up with some tart in town.'

'Poor you!'

Celia watched him get off the bed. Naked, his little wisp of beard looked even more ridiculous. He pulled on his shirt. 'You'll come on Thursday, won't you?'

'I don't know.'

She went into the little bathroom which had been sliced out of the back bedroom, and cleansed herself in cold water; an imposed penance because the immersion heater was off. When she came out Henry had gone. She dressed, folded the sheet and blanket, drew the curtains, returned the mirror to its former position . . .

She went downstairs and out into the sunshine, closed and locked the door and walked to the gate.

'Hullo, Aunt Celia! Been cleaning up for the visitors?'

It was Laura.

Celia looked at her with suspicion and made no reply.

Laura went on, 'I suppose you haven't seen Alice?'

'Alice?'

'Yes, I saw her up on the hill just now but I don't think she saw me.'

Laura fell into step beside Celia and the two women walked back to Nanselow together.

Celia was in the kitchen peeling potatoes for the evening meal; Nancy was seated at the table shelling peas; they were listening to the six o'clock news on the radio. Alice came in.

'I'm going into Truro this evening with Harold to see a film so we shan't be in for the meal.'

Her mother said nothing and Alice went on, 'Is that all right?'

Celia finished peeling a potato and dropped it into a saucepan of water before answering. 'I hope you are not getting too much involved with Harold.'

'I don't know what you mean.'

Celia's voice hardened. 'Of course you know what I mean. It would be a mistake for you to get too fond of him.'

'Why?'

'There are plenty of reasons; he's five years older, he hasn't got a real job and no prospect of getting one; you've got your education and your career to think of.'

'Anything else?'

'Isn't that enough?'

'No, I don't think it is.'

Celia tried to control her irritation. 'At a certain age in growing

84

up a girl is liable to pick up with the first man who happens to be around.'

'Is that what happened to you?'

Celia turned to face her daughter. 'What did you say?'

'Am I the result of your first pick-up or did you have others?'

In a very deliberate manner Celia dropped the knife she was holding and with the whole strength of her arm brought her hand up and slapped her daughter's face.

Alice stood still for a moment, her hand to her cheek which was marked by a muddy streak, then she turned and walked out of the kitchen without a word.

Celia said, 'Oh God! What have I done now? That's the first time I've ever struck her . . .'

Nancy had not stopped shelling peas and the radio babbled on.

Celia was near to tears. 'For a moment I hated her! I could have killed her!' She looked at Nancy, seeking some outlet for her frustration. 'Well, say something, don't just sit there looking so damned superior!'

'What can I say? She upset you and you hit her, it isn't the end of the world.'

There were tears running down Celia's cheeks now and she tried to wipe them away with her wrist. 'All these years . . . and that's where it gets you.'

Nancy said, 'I'm not trying to pry, but does Alice know who her father was?'

Celia snapped. 'No, she doesn't!' And she added after a pause. 'Why?'

'I thought that might explain her attitude. She must feel—'

'I don't care what she feels!' Celia attacked a potato viciously, carving away great pieces. 'And all this in the middle of her A-levels; sometimes I think it's not worth going on.'

In the bus Alice was careful to sit on Harold's left so that he would not see her inflamed cheek; they said little to each other but Harold took her hand in his. They got out at the bottom of Lemon Street and Harold turned back towards the cinema but Alice hesitated.

'I suppose you really want to see this film?'

He looked surprised. 'I thought you did, but I'm not bothered.'

'Shall we go for a walk instead?'

'I'd like that.'

They walked through the town which was almost deserted in the evening sunshine and turned down the road towards Malpas, by the river. When they were clear of the warehouses and builders' yards they were on the edge of the river. It was half-tide and swans cruised on the glassy surface, self-consciously elegantly. Harold put his arm round her and they walked like lovers.

Alice said in a matter-of-fact voice. 'I think it would be a mistake for us to get more friendly than we are.'

She felt him stiffen. 'But why? What—'

'Do you know who my father was?'

'No, but I don't—'

'I don't know either and until I find out I think we should . . . we should be careful not to get involved.'

Harold tried to stop and face her but she continued walking so that he was forced to walk beside her. 'But Alice, I don't care if your father was . . . well . . .'

'If my father was—who were you going to say?'

'Well, anybody. I mean, it just doesn't matter.'

'But what if my father was also yours?'

For a moment Harold was lost for words. 'My— But that's impossible, it's nonsense!'

'Is it? Laura doesn't think so; she put the idea into John's head and he passed it on to me.'

Harold tightened his arm round her waist and tried to draw her to him. 'But darling, that's Laura; she can't help it—'

Alice broke away. 'There's more to it than that. I tackled Laura at lunch time and she said . . .' Alice's voice became uncertain. 'She said, "You don't have to take any notice of me if you don't want to. I haven't got any proof, but if I were you I should think twice."' Alice paused then went on in a rush, 'Do you know that my mother and your father meet at Piper's Cottage in the afternoons?'

Harold said quietly, 'No, I don't know it and I don't believe it. Although Laura is my sister . . .'

'It's not only what Laura says. I went there this afternoon—I know it was spying, but I had to find out for certain. It's true, Harold.'

'But even if it is, that doesn't mean that—'

'No, I know, but we've got to find out.'

Harold said, 'I'll tackle father. I'll ask him outright.'

Alice was moved, knowing what it would have cost him to do that. 'No, I started this and I'll finish it but you'll have to give me time.'

Harold's voice trembled. 'I love you, Alice.'

It was the first time he had said so in so many words and she smiled up at him so that he saw her inflamed cheek.

'Alice! What have you been doing with yourself?'

'Nothing. Mother slapped my face.'

'Slapped . . . But why, for God's sake?'

'I don't know exactly, but I expect I shall find out.'

When they arrived back at the house Alice went straight to her room. Harold expected to find the others just finishing their meal but the old breakfast room was empty and there were no signs that a meal had been served there. He met Nancy in the hall, looking preoccupied and solemn.

She said, 'I thought you and Alice had gone to a film.'

'We changed our minds; is something wrong?'

'They've been on the telephone from Paris; your aunt has had a car smash.'

'Aunt Lucille? Is she badly hurt?'

'I'm afraid so; she's dead.' Nancy looked at him with sudden sympathy. 'I'm sorry to break it to you like this but I'm trying to get Henry off on the night train. They want him over there; you know that he and Lucille were always close.'

He knew too that his aunt had had little to do with her husband's people who had disapproved of the marriage, especially as it had taken place under community property law.

Nancy went on, 'Isobel has gone to the village to break the news to Aunt Constance.'

Aunt Constance was Lucille's and Deborah's aunt and she still occupied the family house in the village, looked after by an ageing housekeeper.

'Does Laura know?'

'No, she's at her society meeting. You could try to get her on the phone. It would be better for her to hear it from you and she might want to go over with your father.'

Harold was finding it difficult to adjust his thoughts which were still concerned with Alice. He succeeded eventually in getting Laura on the line and told her the news. She was silent for a long time, then she said in a tight voice, 'I'll come home straight away.'

Harold was concerned. 'Are you all right?'

'Yes, I'm all right.'

'Are you fit to drive?'

But Laura had replaced her telephone.

The three women were in the kitchen as usual; the clock showed a few minutes after nine. John was at school, Harold had gone to the estate office, but they had not seen Laura.

Celia said, 'She's not going to work.'

But as she spoke Laura came into the kitchen carrying her little bag. She looked ill, her face was drawn and there was scarcely any colour in her cheeks. She had said to Harold the night before, 'It's almost like losing mother over again.'

Without a word she took down her cup and saucer and poured herself some coffee.

Nancy said, 'You don't look well, Laura. Wouldn't it be sensible for you to stay home today?'

'I'm all right but if there is any news from Paris, perhaps you will ring me at the shop.'

She went out and a little later they heard her car being reversed out of the coach house.

Celia poured herself another cup of coffee. 'I thought she would have gone over with Henry.'

Nancy said, 'She's expecting Henry to bring the body home. Apparently Lucille has always said that if she died in Paris she wanted her body brought home for burial.'

Isobel agreed. 'Yes. She told me the same thing last time she was home. She said, "Paris has been good to me, Isobel, but it's not where I belong and it's no place for a woman to grow old in. Before long I shall be packing my bags and coming home for good."'

Celia said, 'But what they do will depend on her will, like a lot of other things.' She sipped her coffee. 'If they bring her home, will they have the funeral from here?'

Nancy looked doubtful. 'I don't know, but I should think so. Aunt Constance couldn't cope.'

Isobel laughed shortly. 'You can say that again!' She lit a cigarette and blew smoke across the table so that Celia coughed ostentatiously. 'When I went over there last night to tell her about Lucille I don't think she took it in. Mrs Treneer says she's only really lucid in the middle of the day. And the house! It's worse than this place. Mrs Treneer does her best but it's a losing battle.'

Celia said, 'But Aunt Constance is well off, she could afford to put the place right and employ people if she wanted to.'

Isobel went on as though Celia had not spoken. 'It's tragic. When I was a girl I used to look at that family with envy and wish that we were like them. The three children, mother, father and Aunt Constance, they were like a story-book family and you never heard a cross word in the house. I've often wondered why Deborah grew up to be like she was. Anyway, Adrian was killed in Korea, mother died a year or two later of a kidney complaint and not long after that father dropped dead in the street. Now there's only Constance left . . .'

Nancy said, 'I must get Ethel's tray or she'll think I've forgotten her.'

'How's she taking it?'

'She was sleeping when I looked in an hour ago.'

Celia started to collect the dirty dishes. 'At that age you stop worrying about anybody but yourself.'

Isobel sat at her desk in the library watching a fly crawl across the paper in her typewriter. It reached the edge of the white paper and stopped, exploring the new surface of the platen with its forelegs and proboscis. Isobel thought, He's not taking any chances, but I'm the biggest threat to his health and happiness and he doesn't even know that I exist.

She was half-way down page forty-nine of her new novel and she was stuck. The eternal triangle had been laboriously constructed and she was searching desperately for some new twist. It was the common theme of all her novels and Payne had once said to her, 'What you need, Isobel, is a new geometry.' She had been hurt and it had put her off writing for several days.

At the moment her strivings were in vain for she could not make herself concentrate. Lucille's death had come as a shock and at a bad time for her peace of mind.

'In two days I shall be fifty!'

The telephone rang and she reached for it. The startled fly took off and flew away.

'Nanselow House.'

'Isobel? It's Tim. I'm ringing from a call-box in the village . . .'

There was no telephone at Tresean and this was the first time she had ever spoken to him on the phone. She made an effort to sound cool.

'Yes, Isobel speaking.'

'I don't know how to put this; it's about my father's gun . . .'

'What about it?'

'It's gone.'

'Gone? Do you mean that somebody has stolen it?'

'I suppose so. It's gone anyway. I can't say exactly when it was taken but the last time I remember seeing it was when you told me I should hand it in. That must be nearly a week ago.'

'It's exactly a week ago. I warned you, Tim.'

'Yes, Isobel, you warned me.'

She could not understand the irony in his voice.

He went on, 'The point is, Isobel, I have to do something about it. I should have reported it already.'

'Yes, and if you don't do it soon you could be in real trouble. Have you spoken to Laura?'

'No.'

'Well, it's up to you. Was there any ammunition with the gun?'

'Yes, some, and that's gone too. I don't know how much there was; it was in a little cardboard carton just as father left it and I've never had the curiosity to look inside.'

He paused, and there was an uncomfortable silence.

'Isobel . . .'

'Yes?'

'You do see that I have to go to the police?'

'Of course! You would be very foolish not to.'

'They will want to talk to you.'

'Then let them talk; they know where I live.'

'Yes. Yes, of course . . . Well, thank you.'

She heard the click as he replaced the telephone. She was puzzled by his manner, then it dawned on her that he believed she had taken his gun.

'Let him think what he likes!'

The police arrived half-way through the afternoon, a sergeant and a woman police constable. Isobel received them in the drawing-room. They were very courteous and correct and, to Isobel's surprise, more than ready to accept her assurance that she had not touched the gun. The sergeant, who looked in need of a square meal, said, 'Only a formality, Miss Care. Only a formality.'

The young policewoman was taking in the decaying elegance of the drawing-room, the patches on the walls where pictures had been, the frayed carpet, the grand piano with a sheen of bluish mould on its polished lid.

'You and your niece are the only members of the family who visit Mr Payne, is that so?'

'Yes.'

'And both of you saw the gun?'

'Apparently. I certainly saw it, and my niece mentioned it one evening at dinner.'

'I gather that you advised Mr Payne to hand the gun over to us.'

'Yes, I did.'

'A great pity that he did not take your advice.'

The sergeant glanced at his notebook. 'The young people in the house—your nephew, John, and Mrs Gilbert's daughter, Alice. I suppose they are at school?'

Evidently the sergeant had done his homework.

'Yes.'

'Would either of them be likely to do this sort of thing as a joke?'

'I'm quite certain they would not; both of them are very sensible and responsible.'

'Yes, of course. What about Miss Laura Care? Would it be possible to have a word with her while we are here?'

'I'm afraid she's not at home but you will find her at her shop—*The Tarot Shop* in Wharf Lane.'

'Oh, *The Tarot Shop*—yes, I know it.' The policeman stood up. 'I don't think we need take up any more of your time, Miss Care . . .'

Isobel saw them to the door and there, under the imposing portico, the sergeant paused. 'Between ourselves, Miss Care, we think we have a pretty good idea where the gun is . . . A troublesome customer we've been keeping an eye on for some time . . .'

They were in the middle of their evening meal when Henry telephoned from Paris. He spoke first to Nancy, then to Laura. Afterwards Nancy told the others what he had said.

'Apparently he's spent most of the day with Lucille's lawyer; he and the lawyer are joint executors under her will. As we thought, she stipulated that her body must be brought home and buried in the village churchyard with the rest of the family. Henry has arranged for her to be flown to Plymouth airport on Friday. He's been on the phone to Nance, the undertaker, and Nance will collect the body from the airport and bring it on by road. It will spend the night in his chapel of rest and the funeral will be on Saturday at three o'clock—at the church, not from here. Nance is looking after all the formalities but we have to tell people who might want to be there . . . Of course, some of them will want to come back here. We shall have to fix up something for them . . . I don't know if he said anything else to you, Laura?'

Laura was looking better, she had more colour and she had eaten what was, for her, a reasonable meal. 'No, I don't think so . . . Oh, yes, there was something. He said he'd forgotten to mention to you about Sunday's open day.'

Nancy groaned. 'I'd forgotten about the blasted open day. Surely, he can't want it the day after the funeral like that?'

'He thinks it should go on because it would be unfair to the Red Cross to cancel it at such short notice.'

Ethel looked across the table at Nancy. 'Did he say anything else about her will?'

'No.'

The old lady sniffed. 'When is he coming back?'

'Sometime on Friday.'

Chapter Five

IT WAS RAINING when Nancy met her husband at the station on Friday afternoon; a steady drizzle which showed no sign of let-up. They met on the platform and Nancy thought he looked very tired; the colour had gone from his cheeks.

'The sun was shining when I left Paris this morning.'

Nancy smiled. 'The sun is always shining when one leaves Paris.'

The old Rover was parked in the station forecourt and she went to get in on the passenger side but Henry stopped her. 'You drive; I've had enough.'

The streets of the town were jammed with holiday-makers driven away from the coasts by the rain. Once clear of the congestion Nancy said, 'What about her will?'

'Apart from a few small legacies everything is to be divided equally between the twins.'

'So she kept her promise. What does everything amount to?'

'I've no idea what they will actually get but Brossier, the lawyer, says that the residue should exceed six and a half million francs.'

'What does that amount to in real money?'

'Three quarters of a million but don't forget that *le percepteur des contributions* will want a very large slice out of that and I'm not sure that our blood-suckers won't come in on the act.'

'All the same, they will be rich.'

Henry laughed without humour. 'The luck of the Cares. Ironic, isn't it?'

'I don't know what you mean.'

'Neither do I. I just wonder what they will do, the pair of them. Harold, on his own, might . . . But what's the good of guessing?

94

They're of age and it will be theirs to do as they like with. In addition Brossier is suing the driver of the other car in a civil action for damages. The man was drunk and there is a criminal prosecution anyway. The heirs wouldn't get much change out of that here but what the position is over there I don't know.'

It was Isobel's birthday and by long established tradition there should have been a party that night but, because of Lucille's death, they had the usual Friday evening dinner followed by a birthday cake with five candles which Henry called a Decimal Cake.

'Laura isn't down.' Henry looked across at Harold.

'No, she's in her room.'

'Is she very upset?'

'Yes, but I think she will be down directly.'

They ate their meal and Isobel cut her cake, then there were presents: cigarettes from Celia, a necklace from Henry and Nancy, a brooch from Ethel. Harold, to Isobel's surprise, turned up with a rather special ball-point. John presented his carved plaque which everyone admired and Alice's gift was a head-scarf.

During the euphoria following the present giving Laura walked in and stood looking at them. 'What's going on? Is this some sort of party?'

Henry said, 'No, not a party, but it's your aunt's birthday.'

The spectacles were turned on him. 'Oh, I'd forgotten. I'm sorry, Aunt Isobel; I suppose I was thinking more about Lucille. It seems an odd time to have a party.' She turned and was walking out of the room.

Nancy said, 'Aren't you having any dinner? There's plenty of food left.'

'No thank you; I don't feel hungry.'

Celia laughed briefly. 'Trust little madam to enter into the spirit of the occasion.'

Harold looked worried.

Henry said, 'She's obviously very upset but that doesn't excuse her rudeness. I'm sorry, Isobel.' He looked round the table uncertainly. 'What about opening a bottle of port? Harold—get out the glasses.'

They drank Isobel's health and the atmosphere once more relaxed. Conversation picked up again.

'How are the exams going, Alice? Nearly over?'

Alice said, 'I've got the second biology paper on Monday, after that just a couple of practicals which I can't do much about in the way of revision.'

'And then—freedom!'

Alice smiled. 'No more school anyway.'

Henry said, 'I seem to have been away a long time but it's only a couple of days.'

Isobel lit a cigarette. 'We had the police here on Wednesday. Perhaps I should say *I* had the police here.'

'Oh? What did they want?'

'Laura told you about Tim Payne's revolver. Well, it's been stolen.'

Henry looked at her sharply. 'I don't like the sound of that! Why did they come here?'

'They wanted to talk to me and to Laura because we both knew about the gun. I think they saw Laura at the shop.'

'Was anything else taken?'

'Apparently not.'

'Surely they don't think that you or Laura—'

'No, I gathered from the sergeant that they suspect somebody or other—somebody they've been keeping an eye on for a long time.'

Henry nodded. 'Saunders and that boy. I wish we could get them out of Tregassick. Saunders is a bad farmer and a bad neighbour. All the same, Payne should have been more careful.'

Harold was on his way to bed when Laura called him into her room. She was wearing a dressing-gown over her nightdress and she was sitting at the little desk by the window on the only chair in the room. She collected her papers and slid them into a drawer.

'Has father spoken to you about Lucille's will?'

'Briefly, yes.'

'What will you do? Will you stay on here?'

'Yes.'

She smiled as though with relief. 'Good! I was afraid you might run out on me.'

'That seems to mean that you will be staying too.'

'Me?' She looked at him in surprise. 'They won't get rid of me.'

'That's all right then.'

Laura stood up, pulling her dressing-gown about her. 'There's something I want to ask you, Harold . . .'

'Well?'

'Don't get annoyed, but have you been in here looking for anything recently?'

Harold was piqued. 'I never come into your room unless you are here.'

'I wouldn't mind if you did.' She smiled at him. 'I don't have any secrets from you, but somebody has been in here, searching through my things.'

'Have you lost anything?'

'No, but I don't like my private things being pawed over by the family.'

'I think you must be mistaken.' He moved towards the door.

'No, don't go!' She picked up two cushions and placed them together by the wall. 'Sit by me for a little while; I've something to tell you.'

They sat side by side and she took his hand in hers. 'You are distant, Harold, and tense. Relax. We mustn't let anything come between us.' She smiled up into his face and he smiled back. 'That's better! Now I can tell you. Earlier this evening I was able to get back once more to that day when mother died.'

'Oh?' Harold's manner was not encouraging.

'Don't look like that! I had to do something or think about Lucille and now that she is gone I am even more determined to find out the truth. I was able to remember much more clearly and in more detail. It was like getting a pair of binoculars properly focused.' She broke off, then went on, 'I remembered that when I wandered off over the rocks I had a spade in my hand—you know those little plastic spades we used for digging in the sand?'

'Yes, I remember.'

'Well, I was carrying mine and when I looked up to the tower and saw them up there I waved with my spade and father waved back.'

'He waved back?'

'Yes and it wasn't he who was standing near mother, it was Nancy. I knew I wasn't seeing it exactly right, my recollection was blurred. It was Nancy who was standing near mother and she was wearing a green dress; she used to wear green a lot then as she still does.'

Laura took off her glasses and her eyes were shining. 'I can see them in my mind so clearly now, just as if I were looking at them. I know exactly how they were standing. Mother was in the embrasure, facing outwards, but I don't think she saw me. Nancy was just behind her and she was reaching out with one arm. Father was on their left, some little way away. I got it wrong at first because I started with a preconceived idea of what had happened and I was trying to force my memories to fit; that's why I wasn't seeing clearly.'

'And you were ready to accuse father of having killed mother. Don't you see that all this is very dangerous and . . . and wrong, Laura? Don't you think you should drop it now before you do—'

She looked at him in a kind of wonderment. 'Drop it? When I am really getting at the truth? Can't you see that Nancy had even more reason to want mother out of the way? She was reaching out to mother—why?'

Lucille Constance Arnaud née Oliver, aged forty-six, was laid to rest in the grave of her mother on Saturday afternoon. Fine, misty rain like a billowing curtain drifted over the churchyard. The whole family was there. Aunt Constance, looking like a corpse herself, stood by the grave supported by Mrs Treneer. People had come from all over the county, some to acknowledge old ties with the Olivers, others out of respect for Henry who was well liked. Lucille's French in-laws were not represented.

Laura and Harold were together throughout the service. Laura's manner was subdued rather than grief-stricken. Henry had tears in his eyes, partly for Lucille, more for the promise of his early life which had somehow failed to materialize. Ethel watched Aunt Constance and there was less than sympathy in that look. Within a month or two they were the same age.

When it was over a few friends returned to the house with the family to eat paté sandwiches which the three women had prepared and drink Madeira which Henry maintained was the only possible drink for a funeral. After they had gone Nancy went up to her room to change. Henry tapped on the door and came in.

'Oh, there you are! I've been looking for you. It went off all right, didn't it?'

'Yes. Very well, I thought.'

Henry sighed. 'Lucille gone! It's hard to believe; I don't think I've really taken it in even now.'

Nancy was zipping up the green satin-jersey dress which she often wore in the evenings. 'Did you want me for something special? You said you'd been looking for me.'

'Yes, I did. I'm a bit worried about Laura; there was that business last night when she was so rude to Isobel, then, this morning, just before lunch, I met her coming out of East Wood carrying a sort of plumber's tool bag. I teased her about it but she wasn't letting on what she was up to.'

'I expect she was coming back from the Prospect Tower. John told me that she's been using the tower for some of her occult experiments or whatever you like to call them.'

Henry looked surprised. 'Really? I had no idea.'

'Was that all?'

'What?—No, that was by the way. The main thing that bothered me was the way she seemed to be brooding on Deborah. I suppose Lucille's death brought it all back but it doesn't seem natural after all these years.'

'What has she been saying?'

'Well, when we met as I said, we walked back to the house together and she started asking me exactly how her mother died.'

'What sort of thing?' Nancy was brushing her long hair in front of the mirror.

'Well, it seems that she's turned up a report of the inquest and she wanted to know if I really thought it was an accident.'

'What did you say?'

'That it was impossible to be sure. I couldn't deny that she might have killed herself. Then she wanted to know about Deborah's mood at the time; what exactly she was doing in the embrasure; what she said, whether her behaviour was different to usual . . . She really interrogated me.'

Nancy was fastening a string of green beads round her neck. She stood up.

Henry said, 'You look beautiful as always. Will you sit for me like that?'

Nancy smiled. 'Not at this minute.'

'No, but sometime when things have settled down again.'

'If you like. What did you tell Laura?'

'What could I tell her? Only that her mother was sometimes very excitable and that this was one of those times. She wanted to know if we had had a row that day and I told her that we hadn't. Then she asked me if I actually saw Deborah fall.'

'And did you?'

Henry looked in surprise at his wife. 'You know that I didn't actually see her fall. I was waving to Laura down on the beach; something made me look and I saw that Deborah had gone and in that same instant I heard an awful thud . . .'

Nancy took her husband's hand. 'Poor Henry! What has always puzzled me is that Laura must have seen her mother fall—she must have done, yet she has never admitted it. How could she possibly not have done?'

Henry sighed. 'I can't imagine, but when I went to the nursery to tell them I could have sworn that she knew nothing.' He hesitated, 'Don't psychologists say that the mind protects itself by shutting out certain memories—repressing them?'

Nancy shook her head. 'It's no good asking me what psychologists say. If you listen to them we are all walking a tightrope between neuroses and psychoses of one sort or another.'

'But what bothers me is that Laura seems to be dwelling on her mother's death still—after sixteen years. Isn't it all a bit abnormal? Morbid?'

Nancy went to the dressing table and picked up her little bag. 'I don't think so. Laura has a romantic view of her mother; she's bound to have—the young and lovely woman whose life ended so tragically and dramatically when her twin children were only six years old. I shouldn't worry about it too much.'

Henry kissed her on the forehead. 'I expect you are right as usual.'

Laura was in one of her more intense moods. Harold had learned to recognize the symptoms and they put him on the defensive. On such occasions her manner was matter-of-fact, brusque. It usually meant that she had rationalized some course of action to her own satisfaction and intended to steam-roller him into agreement.

'I want to do something really creative, Harold.'

It was late evening, the rain had stopped and the sun streamed in through her west-facing window. Laura was half sitting, half lying on her Japanese bed, propped up by cushions and looking a little like a draped odalisque by Ingres.

Harold said nothing.

'In a way, mother's life, and certainly Lucille's, were wasted lives; they were talented and sensitive people but they died unfulfilled. Lucille left nothing of herself behind; mother left us, to be brought up by people who look upon us as encumbrances.'

Harold said, 'What is it you intend to do?'

She turned to face him but the lenses of her spectacles masked her expression. 'I'm going to have a baby.'

'A baby!'

She took off her spectacles and smiled, one of her melting smiles. 'Yes, don't look so shocked.'

'I'm not shocked but are you saying that you are pregnant?'

She laughed. 'Not yet, silly! I'm telling you that I intend to be.'

Harold relaxed and allowed himself to be slightly ironical. 'Do you also intend to get married?'

'Oh no! I shall never marry. I shan't repeat the mistake mother made.'

'But the baby will need a father.'

She shifted impatiently on her cushions. 'What you are saying is that I shall need a man in order to conceive, but there the relationship will end. The baby will be mine. Think of it, Harold! What more creative thing could one do? I don't mean the biological process of producing a child but the work of turning a new-born baby into a *person*. To watch it grow physically, mentally and spiritually and to encourage and *mould* that growth.'

Harold was silent, his sister watched him expectantly for a time, then she said, 'Well? What do you think?'

Harold did not want to say anything at all but he knew that he must. 'I should think about it a lot more before you do anything.'

'I've been thinking about it for a long time already; it was Lucille's death which decided me. It seems like a betrayal to leave nothing of oneself behind.'

Harold got up from where he had been sitting, on a cushion by her bed. 'Surely it's possible that you will find someone and fall in love.'

She laughed. 'Don't be absurd, Harold! I can't stand men and you know it.'

She had succeeded in making him feel thoroughly uncomfortable and helpless as she often did.

'Don't you think it would be . . .' He hesitated, anxious to find a word which would not be too offensive but failed.

'It would be what?'

'Well, degrading, to go around looking for a man to . . . to . . .'

'To service me, that's what you're thinking, isn't it? We might as well use the correct technical term, it exactly defines his function—that and no more.'

Harold was silent.

'I shall need to be very careful. If he is going to contribute anything at all to my child I shall want to be sure that it is something of which I can approve.'

Harold turned on her with more irritation than he had yet

shown, 'Really, Laura, isn't this all a bit weird?'

She was smiling up at him; one of the shoulder straps of her nightdress had slipped exposing a pale breast. 'Of course, it could be you. That would be the ideal solution; then I would have nothing to worry about at all.'

He stood, his hands clenched, glaring at her. 'For Christ's sake, Laura!' He did not know whether she had meant it seriously or as a sick joke but he was more angry with her than he had ever been. He hesitated for a moment longer, seemed on the point of saying something but changed his mind and hurried out of the room.

Sunday morning was fine and warm. Celia dressed carefully in her grey knitted frock with a silver crucifix on a chain round her neck, then she set out for Mass. When Mass was over she went round to the presbytery and asked to speak to Father Bond. The house-keeper put her in the priest's sitting-room which was itself like a little church with its tall Gothic windows which you could not see out of when sitting down.

'Father Bond won't keep you long.' The housekeeper was not the kind of woman one expects to find in a presbytery, she was plump and motherly and given to smiling.

The priest was several years older than Celia, a lean dark man with a permanent five o'clock shadow on his cheeks and chin, thin lips and grey eyes; an Ignatius rather than a Francis.

'Ah, Mrs Gilbert . . .' He noticed Celia's agitation and said less formally, 'Sit down, child, and relax.'

Celia sat on the edge of one of the leather armchairs. 'I am very worried. Alice is demanding to know about her father and I am at my wits' end what to do.'

The priest gave her a quick understanding look. 'Has she asked about him before now?'

'Never . . . I've always rather dreaded that she would but she never has.'

'It was bound to come sooner or later. She must be close to eighteen.'

'She will be eighteen in August.'

'Is she showing interest in some young man?'

'I suppose you could say that. Since her cousin Harold came home she's been going out with him quite a lot.'

The priest frowned and ran his finger between his clerical collar and his thin neck. He seemed to consider carefully what he would say.

'I have not heard your confession for several months.'

Celia flushed. 'No.'

The priest gazed at her, his grey eyes holding hers. 'Are you ready to make your confession now?'

'No, Father, I cannot.'

'The sacrament of penance demands only a contrite heart.'

Celia remained silent and the priest went on, 'Then I must assume that the situation has not changed.'

Father Bond too, lapsed into silence and his long fingers, stippled with black hairs, beat out a tattoo on the polished table top.

'Has it occurred to you that Alice might have discovered something of what is going on?'

Celia stiffened. 'That is impossible!'

The priest smiled. 'My dear Mrs Gilbert, can such secrets be kept? Think about it; if Alice had made such a discovery and, as you say, she has become interested in her cousin . . .'

'Oh, God!' Celia picked at the seams of her grey gloves. 'That's one thing I had never expected to have to face.'

'But you agree that it might be the explanation?'

Celia nodded miserably. 'I've thought of something that happened which makes me think you could be right. Laura, with her poisonous tongue—'

Father Bond stopped her with a gesture. 'You must not lay your own sins on the shoulders of others.'

Celia said, 'But what am I to do, Father?'

The priest looked at her with compassion. 'As to the thing itself, you know what you must do. As to Alice, you must tell her the simple truth.'

'If only she were still in the Church.'

'You did your duty and raised your daughter in the faith; you must not now doubt the power of Christ. Pray, and I will pray for you both.'

'It could ruin her life.'

'Nonsense! You are exaggerating and dramatizing the situation. She will be distressed, but it will pass. In any case, the truth is the same whether she knows it or not and you have no right to keep it from her.'

'I dare not tell her until her exams are over.'

The priest smiled his thin smile. 'No, indeed; that might be unwise.'

On Sunday afternoon Nanselow was open to the public in aid of the Red Cross, with teas provided by the ladies of the local branch. It was a glorious day though rain was forecast for the evening. By three o'clock several hundred people had parked their cars and paid fifty pence each to admire Henry's magnolias, camellias, rhododendrons and azaleas, to watch his fish in their reedy ponds, to explore the sunken garden with its huge and sinister tree ferns, and to walk, if they were so disposed, the four miles of woodland paths all neatly signposted by green arrows supported in split bamboo canes.

For an additional fifteen pence they could buy a booklet about the estate and the family. 'The present house was built in 1820 but the estate has been in the hands of the Care family since the time of James I. Sir William Care was one of the organizers of the defence of Pendennis Castle for the Royalists in 1646 and for this service he was knighted at the Restoration. A baronetcy was conferred on Henry Greville Care by George IV in 1823 and the present Sir Henry Care is the seventh baronet . . .'

Henry, in old gardening trousers and a checked shirt, mingled with his guests taking equal pleasure in being recognized and congratulated or in not being recognized and so overhearing more candid comments about the estate and his family. Henry was sensitive to comment only on the subject of his painting. Ethel and

Isobel promenaded along the paths near the house and made conversation with the visitors. Ethel was dressed in mauve silk while Isobel wore blue chiffon and looked like one of Chagall's levitating ladies who had put on weight.

Nancy, Alice and John were at the nurseries which were open for business, Harold and Laura had not been seen all day and Celia had kept to the house. Celia rarely mixed outside the family, in fact it was unusual for her to leave the estate except to go to Mass and then she did not pass through the village. The villagers had almost forgotten what she looked like. After a more than usually disorganized lunch in the kitchen, she washed up then went to her room to lie on the bed with the *Observer* crossword.

Celia never tired of telling herself and others how much she enjoyed being alone but when she was, she soon became moody and depressed. She filled in a few words of the puzzle then lost interest; she read the reviews and the women's pages then she let the paper slip to the floor. She did not sleep but lay on her back staring up at the pattern of cracks in the ceiling. Her window was open and she could hear the subdued murmur of voices, the occasional shout or burst of laughter from the visitors. Most of them tended to congregate near the house. She had often watched them on open days; some of them peered unashamedly in at the ground-floor windows; others, more circumspect, walked slowly past, seeing what they could. There was a great deal of interest in how 'the family' lived. If only they knew! In a semi-detached on a housing estate you don't have to place chamber-pots and bowls strategically when it rains or deal with rats in the cellars.

'And what do I get out of it? I have no more rights here than a housekeeper.'

She turned on her side, face to the wall. 'Other people have troubles but there can't be many women of my age so alone in the world. Alice has grown away from me; she is positively antagonistic, and when she goes there will be no-one.'

Laura put on the blue silk dress which she had worn the previous Sunday and set out for Tresean. She made her way across the park, ignoring the groups of visitors who looked after her with knowledgeable eyes. 'She's the daughter by his first wife; she runs that fortune telling shop in Wharf Lane and they say she's a bit strange.'

She found Payne working in his room, surrounded by books and papers, but he greeted her warmly. She noticed that he was wearing a fawn shirt and slacks which set off his slim figure and made him look younger; she guessed that this was for her.

'I thought you had decided not to come; I'd almost given you up.'

She stood by his desk, looking down at his papers and books which were mostly in German.

'What were you doing?'

'I was working on my book.'

'But what, exactly?'

He smiled. 'I've been drafting the chapter on the philosopher, Fichte; in particular the section dealing with his supposed influence on the growth of the cult of the state in Germany.'

She made a dismissive gesture with her long delicate hands. 'Ideas—all the time ideas! Aren't you interested in people? This man, Fichte, did he have a wife? Mistresses? Children? Did he have nasty little vices that he wrote about in his diary?'

Payne laughed. 'He certainly had a wife; he died of typhus which he caught while nursing her. I doubt if he went in for mistresses or colourful vices; he seems to have been a model of rectitude though he was accused of atheistic tendencies.'

'A very dull man; I doubt if I shall read your book.'

'I sometimes wonder whether anybody will read my book. You want me to go in for candid biography. Perhaps I should, there's a great deal more money in it.'

Laura looked round the room. 'Where is your cat?'

Payne thought, Damn her! She deliberately refuses to show a glimmer of interest in anything I say. Aloud, he said, 'I expect she's in the garden at the back; she has a routine—mornings in here with me, afternoons in the garden either sleeping or stalking field mice.'

'Sensible creature! Shall we sit out there as we did last week?'

'Of course! The chairs are already there in case madam felt so inclined.'

Not only were the chairs in place but the jungle had been pushed back. Payne had been active with scythe and mower.

They sat side by side in the old steamer chairs, the canvas of which was bleached almost white. She sat with her pale thighs exposed but he resisted the temptation to touch her.

She said, 'I had the police at the shop asking me about your gun.'

'Yes, I'm sorry about that. I hope they didn't bother you.'

'No, they didn't bother me. Are you in trouble?'

'I am to be prosecuted on two charges under the Firearms Act.'

'What will they do to you?'

'Well, they could send me to gaol for six months but I don't think they will. My solicitor thinks it will cost me a couple of hundred pounds in fines.'

'Spiteful.'

'On the part of the police?'

'No, I was thinking of whoever took the wretched thing.'

'The police think that it was Dippy Saunders; they didn't say so in so many words but they made it fairly obvious.'

'Is that what you think?'

He was guarded, 'I suppose it's possible.'

'It doesn't seem very likely to me.'

He could see her in profile, her lips were parted, her teeth glistened, and while he watched, her pointed little tongue explored the whole contour of her lips with narcissistic satisfaction. His experience of a week ago had taught him something. He thought, Sex is her weapon. But the dew is already gone, when the bloom follows she will need to look out for herself.

He said, 'Shall we go inside?'

'No, I like it here.'

'Would you like a cold drink?'

'No, thank you.' She was lying back with her eyes closed. The canopy of the chair cast a shadow which reached her shoulders. For a long time neither of them spoke. Payne wondered if they would end up in the bedroom and if they did whether she would try to humiliate him once more. If so he was ready for it.

In the end she said, 'Do you think intelligence is inherited?'

He tried not to sound pedantic. 'I don't know but one certainly gets that impression. If one thinks of the Cecils and the Churchills, the Darwins and the Huxleys . . .'

Chapter Six

TWO MONTHS AFTER Lucille's funeral: on the face of it, life at Nanselow had returned to normal. The three women breakfasted daily in the kitchen and Henry had resumed his painting though, finding water too difficult and haystacks unsympathetic, he had forsaken Monet and was now concentrating on painting and repainting the view from his studio window after the manner of the various impressionists and post-impressionists he admired. Alice had finished school and was waiting for the results of her A-levels, while John was on holiday and both of them were spending a good deal of their time at the nursery to earn a little money. Harold, now established in the estate office, had acquired a new air of gravity and purpose. He consorted with the tenant farmers, attended the Wednesday cattle market and read books on animal and plant husbandry and woodland management.

Celia said, 'Alice's results should be out. They said on or before the fifteenth of August and it's the fourteenth today. It wouldn't surprise me if she'd already had them and kept quiet. She's scarcely spoken to me since . . .'

Isobel was spreading margarine on toast, part of her new slimming diet which, she insisted, had economic rather than aesthetic aims. 'Otherwise I shan't be able to wear anything I possess.'

The day was overcast with a dry wind from the east; what the weathermen call anti-cyclonic gloom. The clock on the wall showed eight minutes past nine.

Nancy said, 'Laura is late this morning.'

As she spoke, Laura came in and took down her cup and saucer from one of the tall cupboards. 'Is there any coffee?' She opened another of the cupboards, 'I thought there were some cornflakes.'

Nancy said, 'Top shelf.'

They watched her help herself to cornflakes and milk and add milk to her coffee.

Miss Pearl arrived with the post. 'Good morning, Lady Care . . . Good morning! Such a *gloomy* morning; I do so dislike this east wind . . .' She cleared a space on the plastic cloth and laid out the envelopes; Celia went to stand by her side.

'Four for Sir Henry—one from Paris; three for Lady Care; five for Miss Isobel. Mr Harold has had his at the office. And one for Miss Alice.'

Celia snatched at the buff envelope with its typewritten address. 'Do you think I should take it up to her?'

Isobel said, 'I wouldn't if I were you; I should leave it here for when she comes down.'

Celia gazed at the envelope as though she had some hope of penetrating its contents. 'Everything depends on her grades— *everything*.'

'What does she need?'

'King's have offered her a place with three Bs; Liverpool will take her with two Bs and a C.'

Laura finished her cornflakes and picked up her little bag. A moment or two later they heard her driving out of the yard.

Isobel said, 'What's come over her? She actually ate a spoonful of cornflakes. It must be a feast day.'

Alice came in, she was wearing an old pair of slacks and a flowered top from which most of the colour had bleached out; her hair was unbrushed and she had a sulky expression. Isobel thought, My God! Youth can get away with murder.

Her mother said, with tension in her voice, 'Your results have come, Alice,' and she pointed to the buff envelope.

Alice glanced at it and said, 'Oh, somebody's been having cornflakes. Is there enough milk?'

She tipped some cornflakes into a bowl, added milk and sat down to eat them.

'Aren't you going to open it?' Celia's expression was agonized.

Alice took the envelope, looked at the address then picked up a knife and slit it open. She took out the slip of computer print-out, glanced at it and stuffed it into the pocket of her slacks.

'Well? What did you get?'

She was sprinkling sugar on her cornflakes. 'Oh, I did all right.'

'But your grades, Alice—what were your grades?'

'I got three As.'

'Three As! But that's absolutely marvellous!' Celia was in a sudden transport of delight. 'Wonderful! Isn't that wonderful, Nancy?'

'Yes, I should think it was.'

Tears were running down Celia's cheeks. 'I'm so pleased I don't know what to do. Now you'll be able to send off the slip saying you accept.'

Alice was eating her cornflakes without looking up. She said nothing.

'Won't you?'

'Won't I what?'

'Be able to send off your acceptance slip for King's.'

'I suppose so. I don't know.'

'But you don't want to go to Liverpool, do you?'

'No.'

'Well, then . . .'

'I shall have to think about it.'

Celia stood for a moment transfixed, staring at her daughter; her hands were clasped tightly together and her expression was totally incredulous. In the end she burst out, 'Damn you! Damn you! You can go on the streets for all I care!' And Celia rushed out of the room.

Alice continued with her cornflakes and Nancy said, 'You could try to be a bit more understanding with your mother, Alice.'

Alice swept her hair back from her eyes. 'I don't like being treated like a performing seal. "For her next trick Sadie will balance on the ball and play *God Save the Queen* on the trumpets."'

'You could explain.'

'You try explaining anything to my mother.'

Nancy collected her dishes and took them over to the sink. 'I'll get Ethel's tray.'

*

At supper that night Henry said, 'We will open a bottle of wine.'

Isobel said, 'But it's only Thursday.'

'I know, but we'll toast Alice—three A-levels with A grades in all of them surely deserves a litre of semi-sweet, blended plonk from the EEC wine-lake.' He grinned at Alice. 'It's worth champagne but the butler forgot to chill it.' Henry always showed a special kindness toward Alice.

They drank the toast and emptied the bottle which, split between eight, scarcely made an orgy. (Laura did not take alcohol.) When the main course was over and they had reached dessert Laura said in a quiet yet hard voice, enunciating each syllable, 'Somebody is making a habit of searching my room; it has happened several times in the past few weeks but until today, nothing has been taken.'

Henry looked at his daughter with apprehension, wondering what was coming next. 'Why should anyone want to search your room?'

'I've no idea, but today something was taken and I want it back.'

Nancy said, 'Surely, Laura, you must be mistaken. What have you lost?'

Laura cleared her mouth of strawberry mousse before replying. 'I am not mistaken. Something has been taken and whoever took it will not need to be told what it was. I want it back.'

There was an uncomfortable hush as Laura continued to spoon up her mousse.

Ethel said, as only Ethel could, 'If you are ashamed to say what it was, then perhaps it's as well that you've lost it.'

Laura looked up sharply but changed her mind; she knew better than to tangle with the old lady.

After one or two false starts, Nancy succeeded in getting conversation going again, with a story about a customer at her nursery who insisted that she wanted synthetic horse manure.

Afterwards Alice was lying on her bed reading a novel. Of all things it was a dog-eared copy of Wells's *Ann Veronica* which she had found on the shelves in the old butler's pantry. To her astonishment she discovered a bond with this Edwardian girl to an extent that brought stinging tears to her eyes. Ann Veronica had wanted to escape too. But the irony of it was not lost on Alice. 'She wanted to escape into the very world which I am trying to escape from.' Or so it seemed.

There was a tap on the door and her mother came in looking pale and long suffering. Celia shivered. 'It seems very chilly in here, don't you think you ought to have a little electric heater?'

Alice thought, This is it! She sat up and swung her legs over the side of the bed. Something inside her seemed to shrivel.

Celia said, 'We can't go on like this, Alice. It's your birthday on Monday, you'll be eighteen . . . I'd like to think that before then we were on better terms . . .' She sat in the little tub chair by the window so that Alice saw her only in silhouette against the greyness outside. Alice thought, This is like one of those television interviews where one of the parties doesn't want to be identified.

Celia said, 'I think all this is partly my fault, perhaps it's all my fault—I just don't know. I should have told you certain things earlier but they are difficult things to talk about and, in any case, mothers always refuse to believe that their daughters are grown up.'

Alice thought, She is going to tell me intimate things about herself which she does not want to tell me and I do not want to hear. All I want to know is who my father was but she will try to explain . . . She wondered why any intimacy between her mother and herself was so intensely embarrassing for both of them.

Celia went on, 'I was twenty when I first met your father and I was working for a firm of solicitors in Holborn. He was twenty-eight, a junior partner in a firm of accountants with offices in the same building.'

Alice experienced a great wave of relief.

Her mother went on, oblivious. 'His name was Alan Dwyer; he was a very quiet young man, he kept himself to himself and he was shy, so shy that he blushed when people spoke to him . . . We met because we went to the same place for lunch and because we were two singles we often found ourselves sharing a table. I could see that he had never had much to do with girls and I had never met anyone like him before. He was very intelligent but terribly unsure of himself, always apologizing. I used to tease him about it until I realized that it upset him. He was so sensitive—so very easily hurt.'

Alice was astonished by the tenderness in her mother's voice.

'We started to go out together in the evenings—concerts and plays—all fairly highbrow. It was a long time before he even touched me, before we ever kissed. I had a bedsitter in a little street off Queensway and he lived with his parents in Camden.'

Celia turned to face her daughter, her eyes bright with tears. 'One evening in the autumn of 1960, when we had been going about together for about three months, he said that before we got any closer there was something he had to tell me. It turned out that some years before he had experienced what is called a manic episode and for three days he had gone about spending money like water, running into debt, accosting girls in the street, frequenting pubs and behaving like a totally different person. He had spent some time in hospital and had continued treatment after returning to work. Although there had been no signs of a recurrence the doctors had warned him that there would probably be other attacks though they were more likely to be depressive than manic . . .'

Celia broke off and turned away to wipe her eyes with a rolled-up handkerchief. 'The attack began that Christmas. Alan was moody and depressed all through the holiday; he started to accuse himself of being insensitive and selfish in allowing me to continue a relationship with a man who was mentally ill. One moment he was begging me to go away and forget him, the next he was saying that if I ever left him he would kill himself.'

For a moment Celia was too overcome to continue. Alice waited, sitting on her bed, rigid and tense, dreading the denouement and wishing that anything might happen to prevent her hearing about it. But her mother's voice resumed implacably.

'I tried to persuade him to go into hospital but he wouldn't and his parents were no help; they were more concerned with assuring everybody that their son was not mentally ill.'

Celia looked straight at her daughter and waited, forcing her to raise her eyes.

'It was then that we made love for the first and only time; one evening in my room. Shortly afterwards Alan became much worse and he was forced to go into hospital. Under treatment he improved rapidly and there was talk of him coming home again but he had a sudden relapse and he hanged himself in one of the lavatories.'

Alice shivered as though the room had become suddenly cold.

'By that time I knew that I was pregnant but I had not told him.'

The silence lengthened and became unbearable. In the end Alice said in a harsh voice, 'I am sorry, mother.'

'What for? For being born?' Celia reached out to touch her daughter's shoulder but her hand stopped short of contact. 'Apart from the priest, Henry is the only one who knows what I have just told you. I went to him in desperation and he took me in; not even Deborah could stop him.' She hesitated, watching the girl. 'Since then I have tried in various ways to make it up to him.'

In her mind Alice could see a dingy, over-furnished room with a gas-fire burning and the curtains drawn. On a narrow bed her mother was making love to a strange man, thin, black-haired and bonily naked. She thought, That is how I began.

She said, 'Why didn't you get rid of me?'

'*Alice!*'

'Didn't you think of it?'

Celia hesitated. 'Not for long.'

Alice swept back the dark hair from her face. 'Of course, that was before it was legal, and in any case you were a Catholic.'

Celia stood, looking down at her daughter, guilty, puzzled and humiliated. 'Do you have to be so bitter?' And when Alice did not answer she added after a moment or two, 'I've got a photograph of your father; would you like to see it?'

'No!' She had the greatest difficulty in repressing a shudder for she had the absurd notion that if she saw the picture it would be that of a pallidly naked man. 'No, thank you. I'd rather not.'

Her mother said, not moving, 'I'll go now—leave you to think it over. I hope it hasn't upset you too much . . . If there's anything you want to ask me . . .'

'No, there's nothing.' She had been told more than she wanted to know already.

Celia went out slowly, hoping that Alice might call her back.

'Do you intend to stay at home now?'

They were sitting on the edge of the quay after swimming, legs dangling.

'It depends on father. I must admit I've got interested and when Aunt Lucille's will is settled I could do something. There should be enough to put the house in reasonable shape and to help the tenants to modernize their farms so that we can get better rents. Then I think Nancy would like to launch out into market gardening which could be profitable if we had enough capital.'

Alice looked at him and smiled. 'You've changed.'

He smiled back. 'Have I? Not in one thing.'

The invisible barrier. Alice had been avoiding him in recent weeks and when they were together there was a constraint. Swimming today there had been no tangling of legs under water, no wandering hands, no wet kisses.

Alice said, 'Mother has been telling me things.'

He waited as a patient waits when the doctor says, 'I've had your report . . .'

She spoke in the manner of someone reciting something very boring which has been learnt by heart. 'My father was an accountant called Alan Dwyer who worked in the same building as my mother. He was twenty-eight, clean-living, hard-working and incredibly dull. His intentions were tediously honourable and he laid mother only once. Unfortunately he was a manic-depressive and he had to go into a mental hospital for treatment. Just when they thought he was getting better he hanged himself in a lavatory.

'Of course, the poor man didn't know that he was due for a half-share in me and he hadn't got round to marrying mother.'

Harold took her hand, his whole being flooded with a sense of

117

enormous relief. 'Alice! Don't talk like that.'

'Perhaps you don't know what manic-depression is—I didn't until I looked it up in the library when I was in town this morning.'

Harold squeezed her hand, 'I don't want to know what it is; it doesn't make any difference.'

She pulled her hand away. 'Of course it makes a difference! It said in the encyclopaedia that a manic-depressive is liable to unpredictable fits of depression with suicidal tendencies and it went on: "statistics suggest a hereditary predisposition to the disorder which often appears for the first time in young adults."'

They stopped talking while one of the Falmouth pleasure boats packed with trippers cruised up-river past them. A disembodied voice reached them across the water: 'On your left you have the famous King Harry Ferry—this is a chain ferry . . .'

Alice said, 'That means it's hereditary.'

'That's not what you said; you said something about a statistical hereditary predisposition.'

'That's playing with words. Whatever you call it, it means that I could be affected at any time, tomorrow, next week or next year.'

Harold said with unusual sharpness. 'You know it's absurd to talk like that!'

She ignored him. 'And if I escape, any children I had would be at risk. You think of having children and watching them grow up, wondering all the time how long it will be before—'

'Before they are run over by a bus or fall off a cliff or get bitten by a mad dog.'

'Be serious, Harold!'

'I am serious. I'm sure it isn't like you say.' He hesitated, then went on with a rush, 'When you talk like that, you sound like Laura.'

'Like Laura!' That surprised her. 'In what way?' She was making up her mind whether to be offended.

'It's just that Laura dramatizes things.'

'And that's what I'm doing, is it?'

'In a way, yes. Anything anybody ever does is a risk of some sort.'

Alice stood up and put on a wrap-over frock over her bikini. 'Yes, well, we shall have to see.'

Harold pulled on his trousers. 'It's your birthday on Monday.'

'Yes, they told me.'

'Eighteen. You'll be a woman—official.'

'Big deal!'

Lunch on Sunday was the usual catch-as-catch-can affair in the kitchen. Nancy was at the nursery where a fine August Sunday boosted the sale of plants doomed to unseasonable transplantation and an early death. Laura was not around. Otherwise the family was complete and chairs were at a premium. Henry lolled against the ancient but massive refrigerator and watched Alice with comfortable domesticated lust. She wore a flimsy, wrap-over sleeveless frock and very little underneath; her skin was lightly, deliciously browned, her dark hair hung down to her shoulders and hid one side of her face. There she was, totally unselfconscious, eating cracker biscuits and cheese.

Henry said, in all innocence, 'Looking forward to King's?'

Celia looked up sharply, first at Henry, then at her daughter.

'I don't know if I shall be going there yet.'

'With three As?'

Celia said, 'She got three distinctions; she never even mentioned that. I wouldn't have known if her year tutor hadn't rung up. She'll get a prize from the examining board.'

Henry grinned, 'Money?'

Alice grinned back. 'Hope so.'

'King's will roll out the red carpet.'

The grin vanished. 'We shall have to see.'

Isobel held up a pot of salad dressing that was nearly empty. 'Does anybody want any more of this? If not I'll finish it up . . .'

Ethel chuckled, 'Part of this famous slimming diet we hear so much about?'

Harold said, 'Where is Laura? I haven't seen her all day.'

John was finishing the remains of a cold bread pudding. He looked across to Harold and Alice and said, diffidently, 'I thought

I'd take the dinghy out this afternoon; I don't know if you two would care to come?'

Harold looked pleased but turned to Alice. Alice said, 'I don't mind.'

Isobel said, 'I'm taking mother over to see Aunt Constance, Celia. We shall be back about five—plenty of time to give you a hand with the dinner.'

Henry thought, It's amazing! We are beginning to sound like a family.

By three o'clock the house was empty except for Celia in the kitchen and Henry in his studio. Henry wore his working rig—a khaki shirt and denim trousers held up with old fashioned braces, the whole ensemble stained with every colour in the Methuen handbook. His studio occupied the south-east corner of the first floor. 'No north-light nonsense for me!' And he worked at an easel near the window on another version of the view over the park.

'Celia!' He had heard Celia's footsteps in the corridor. 'Come in and tell me what you think of my picture.'

'I'm going up to my room to lie down for an hour.'

'You can do that afterwards.'

Celia entered the large bare room which had canvases stacked round the walls. There were plaster casts which were never used, a lay-figure, and a draped couch dating from the days when Henry had employed a model.

He stood back critically from his work. 'What do you think?'

Celia looked without enthusiasm. 'It's a pleasant picture.'

'In whose style?' He faced her, his astonishingly blue eyes, eager and anxious.

'Is it the chap who painted in little dots—the pointillist, I can't remember his name.'

'Seurat—no, it isn't Seurat but you are close. It's in the style of one of Seurat's disciples, Pissarro. You see, they're little dabs with the brush like the tip of a flame, and they're not pure colours. But the effect is obtained in the same way—by apposition . . .' He broke off. 'My grandfather knew Pissarro—and Renoir, and he met Monet once or twice. I remember him telling me that as a young man he could have bought as many Pissarros as he wanted for a few hundred francs a time . . .'

He made a few jabs at the canvas then turned to Celia again. 'You look peaky, Celia; I thought so at lunch. What's the matter? Something bothering you?'

'It's Alice.'

'Alice! I thought she'd done marvellously. Must be a genius. What more could you want?'

'I think she's made up her mind not to go to medical school and I wouldn't be surprised if she's decided not to go to university at all.'

'Really? But why? Does she give any reason?'

'She never gives me any reason for anything; lately she scarcely even speaks.'

Henry put down his brush and put his arm round Celia's shoulders. 'My poor Celia! I'll bet it's something quite silly. Girls at that age get daft notions into their heads. I remember old Leggy Charlton having similar trouble with his girl a year or two back. When his wife finally got it out of her what it was all about, it turned out that she thought it was the "done thing" to go to bed with the male students—almost part of the curriculum—and she didn't fancy it.' Henry chuckled. 'I'll bet the little hussy soon changed her mind when she got there.'

Somehow Celia found herself sitting on the couch with Henry beside her.

'You must sit for me in the nude, Celia; you've got a wonderful body and nobody but me ever sees it.'

Celia was under no illusion about where this was supposed to lead. 'That's over, Henry. I've made peace with my conscience and I've been to confession.'

'So you've decided to become a nun at thirty-five.'

Celia was wearing a blouse and slacks and Henry's hand was massaging her back under her blouse and brassière straps.

'I'm thirty-eight as you well know and I'm not becoming a nun, I've simply decided not to share Nancy's husband.'

But Henry was practised in the art of seduction and by easy stages, without forcing the pace, he persuaded Celia to allow him to undress her and it was at this point that the front door-bell rang, a jangling sound which echoed through the house.

Celia sat up, guilty and embarrassed, as though the bell had awakened her conscience. 'Who the hell is that?' Unexpected visitors were rare at Nanselow.

'It doesn't matter. Let them ring, they'll soon get tired.'

A second peel followed before the first had died away and Celia got off the couch to grope on the floor, naked, for her pants. 'There's something wrong, I can feel it.'

She dressed frantically and tried to tidy her hair with her fingers. 'Damn you, Henry! Why did you have to start this?' She was scared now that whoever it was would go away before she could get down but the ringing persisted.

Henry said, hopefully, 'I'll wait for you.'

Celia mustered what dignity she could on her way down the stairs and took a quick look at herself in the pier-glass in the hall before opening the big frosted glass door which separated the hall from the vestibule.

'Yes?'

She was faced with a couple of teenagers, dressed almost identically in bush jackets and shorts and with unisex hairstyles, but certain curves of figure and feature differentiated girl from boy with tolerable certainty.

'What do you want?'

For the young couple stood there, flushed and breathing hard and looking scared. Finally the girl blurted out, 'Up there by the tower there's a girl.' She pointed vaguely in the direction of East Wood.

And the boy added, 'We think she is dead.'

Celia said in a flat voice, 'What does she look like?'

'She's blonde—I think I've seen her before. I think she's the girl from that queer shop in Wharf Lane.'

The boy said, 'She's wearing a sort of white cloak with stars and things on it . . .'

'But she's almost naked.'

Celia felt cold inside and wondered if she was going to faint. She looked at the two youngsters standing there, waiting expectantly for this adult to tell them what to do, and she thought, What do I do?

She did not say this aloud but the boy seemed to answer her thought. 'We thought there ought to be a doctor . . . Or the police . . .'

'The *police*?'

'Well, I mean, something may have happened to her.'

He meant that she could have been raped and murdered. Young people are brought up on a diet of such possibilities.

Celia said, 'Oh, God!' and then, 'Come inside and wait, I'll . . . I'll get someone.'

She went back upstairs to Henry's studio where Henry, looking ridiculous in his shirt, was studying his painting. 'Well? Who was it?'

'It's Laura I think. Two youngsters say that she's lying up there by the Prospect Tower . . .'

'Well?' Henry was looking at her wild-eyed.

'They think she's dead, Henry.'

Henry said nothing but cast about for his trousers and dragged them on.

'Where are you going?'

'I'm going up there. Get Fox on the telephone and tell him to join me. You'd better send somebody up the drive to show him how to get there.'

She followed him down the stairs and through the hall and watched him as he set off across the park in his painting rig without even a jacket. She was experiencing a tremendous inertia; she felt like someone under sedation being forced to do things for which she had neither the will nor the strength. Then she saw the two youngsters standing in the hall and wondered, for an instant, what they were doing there.

'Is there anything we can do?' The girl looked at her anxiously.

'No—yes, there is. Do you know the way from the drive gates to the tower? Is that how you got there—down the little lane?'

'Yes.'

'The doctor will be coming. If you meet him at the gates and take him down the lane he will have to leave his car where the lane ends just beyond the cottage. From there he will have to walk as you did.'

They went and Celia felt relieved. Now she had to ring Dr Fox. In the library she fumbled through the list of numbers they commonly called. Dr Fox . . . She dialled, got an answering service and was referred to another number—Dr Lobb's.

'Dr Lobb?'

'Dr Lobb speaking.'

She explained as coherently as she could.

'Did you say Miss Laura Care?'

'Yes. The youngsters who found her will be at the gates to show you where to go and Sir Henry will be there before you.'

Henry had said nothing about phoning the police. She telephoned the nursery and asked to speak to Nancy. Nancy would know what to do.

Henry climbed the steep slope to the promontory, driving himself with a sense of blind urgency, and by the time he reached the plateau his heart was racing and he had difficulty with his breathing so that he was forced to stop. He did so for just long enough to recover his breath and relieve the crippling stitch in his side. He could see the tower, the window and part of the door, but he could not see Laura. He had not expected to, he knew that he would find her where his wife had fallen. He was living again that instant of time when he had seen just space where Deborah had stood and heard that thud which was like no other sound he had ever known. There had been no scream, no long-drawn-out harrowing cry—nothing.

Then he had looked down, and there she was, sprawled on the grass at the foot of the tower, her orange dress up round her waist. In the early days of their marriage he had often seen her like that, sprawled on the bed, watching him through half-closed lids.

Now it was his daughter, but no orange dress. One of Deborah's sandals had come off in the fall and they had found it later, caught in a bramble bush, but both Laura's feet were bare. In fact, she was shockingly, obscenely naked, for the white embroidered robe, caught with a cord about her neck, had billowed away from her body as she fell. Henry stooped and clawed at it frantically, doing his best to cover her. His hand came into contact with the pale flesh and he snatched it away as though burned—her flesh was cold as charity.

He stood up, tears blinding him. 'My poor child!' He fiddled with his absurd little beard and his lips trembled. 'My poor child!' He looked up at the tower and his lips moved soundlessly.

Dr Lobb found him standing there. Lobb was a youngish man with curly red hair going thin on top. Henry looked at him with clouded uncomprehending eyes.

'Lobb! Where's Fox?'

'We have a rota at weekends, Sir Henry.'

Henry felt, obscurely, that this was wrong. Fox should have been there as he had been for Deborah. Sixteen years ago this young fellow had been at school—at most, in his first year at medical school.

Lobb bent over the body. Henry did not watch, he moved away to the edge of the clearing and stared out at the estuary. The next thing he knew Lobb was beside him.

The doctor said quietly, 'It seems that she fell from the top of the tower.'

Henry looked at him with an expression of such intensity that the man shifted uncomfortably and muttered something which sounded like an apology.

'The young people who brought me here; I asked them to do the same for the police . . .'

'The *police?*'

'I notified them; it's usual in the case of a fatal accident.' In fact the doctor's caution had been due to a reference by Celia to the young people having said that the girl was nearly naked. Lobb had no intention of being on the receiving end of any official brick-bats.

The police came; a uniformed constable and a sergeant.

Afterwards Henry could not have said whether or not he had heard the laconic exchanges between the doctor and the policemen which were couched in low tones and discreet language out of consideration for him.

The doctor said, 'She's been dead a long time. It's coming up for five o'clock, I'd say she's been here since sometime last night.'

'I suppose there's no doubt that she died as a result of falling from the tower, doctor?'

Lobb was caustic. 'If you can think of a more reasonable explanation of multiple fractures . . . But what was she doing up there in this rig-out?'

Another police voice, the constable, said, 'She ran that shop in Wharf Lane next to Trevail's antiques and I suppose she was interested in all this witchcraft business.'

'Her face is a funny colour; I'd like Dakin to see her.'

'The pathologist? You're not suggesting, doctor—'

'I'm not suggesting anything except that I'd like Dakin's opinion . . .'

'That will be up to the coroner.'

One of the policemen spoke at length on his personal radio.

'They're sending transport and notifying the coroner. I suppose there's no reason why we shouldn't shift her?'

Lobb said, 'Not from my point of view but shouldn't we take a look up there?' He indicated the top of the tower.

Henry became aware of the sergeant standing beside him. 'Excuse me, Sir Henry, this is a terrible experience for you. If you don't feel up to answering a few questions we can always—'

'I'd rather get it over.'

'Just the bare facts for the coroner's office, sir. The young lady's name?'

'Laura Oliver Care—Oliver was her mother's maiden name.'

'And of course you identify her as your daughter. How old was she, sir?'

'Twenty-two.'

'And she lived at Nanselow. I won't keep you much longer. I understand that the young lady's mother died many years ago . . .'

'Sixteen years.'

'Now, Dr Lobb thinks that the accident must have occurred sometime during the night; is it likely that she would have been up here in the middle of the night, sir?'

Henry looked at him blankly. 'I'm sorry. What did you say?'

The sergeant repeated his question.

'I don't know. She was interested in everything to do with the occult and she was probably carrying out some experiment or ritual.'

'You didn't know that she was up here last night, sir?'

'Of course I didn't.'

'It must have been pretty scary for a young woman alone.'

'That wouldn't have bothered Laura.'

'I see, thank you, Sir Henry. I don't think I need trouble you any more. We want to take a look at the top of the tower but there is no need for you—'

'I shall come with you.'

'There is really no need, sir.'

'I want to see.'

Henry insisted on leading the way up the winding stone steps to the top of the tower where he had not been in all the sixteen years since Deborah's death. The steps were barely wide enough for the constable who had to negotiate them sideways.

Out on the leaded roof the scene was strangely pathetic in the light of day. The vermilion lines of the pentagram and the double circle were rather shakily drawn on the scaly lead and there were only greasy red smears to mark where candles must have stood at the five points of the pentagram. Two brightly painted wooden wands, a dagger and a sword, looked like toys left behind by a careless child. There was a small copper brazier containing grey ash and some unburnt herbs as well as a small wooden box wound about with a strand or two of iron wire. The box was barely singed.

The policeman looked round in astonishment while the doctor poked about in the brazier raising a cloud of dust. 'Do you think we could collect some of this stuff in a plastic bag?'

The sergeant rescued the little wooden box and slid off the binding wire. Inside there was a yellowish-grey powder and a piece of very stiff paper or parchment.

'There's something written on it—"Beelzebub".' He turned to Henry. 'I don't suppose you can tell us what all this is about, sir? Or if she's done anything like this before?'

Henry tugged at his beard. 'I don't know. This is all new to me. I had no idea what kind of thing she did—no idea.'

The constable was standing in one of the embrasures, looking down. He said, quietly, to his colleague, 'She must have fallen from this one, sarge, and look . . . just here on the slate, there's an inscription—"Deborah Care 1963. Aged 26." It's like an inscription on a headstone.'

The sergeant looked across at Henry with diffidence. 'Could you tell us this, sir? It seems to have been done fairly recently.'

Henry walked over and looked down at the slate. 'I've never seen it before.'

'But you know what it means?'

Henry's lips were quivering. 'It marks the spot where my wife—my first wife, fell to her death sixteen years ago.'

'And who do you think carved the inscription, sir?'

'It must have been Laura; no-one else would have done it.'

The sergeant and the constable exchanged glances. As far as they were concerned they had the answer. All wrapped up.

The sun was abruptly hidden by thin grey mist and out to sea, clouds which had been building all the afternoon were moving landwards.

The women were in the drawing-room. Because of what had happened people would 'come' and one can't receive visitors in the kitchen. Despite the sunshine all day the air in the room was chilly and damp which probably explained why the piano grew blue mould on its polished surfaces and why it had been impossible to tune for years.

Ethel was wearing a knitted shawl over her mauve silk dress and Isobel had on her blue chiffon. The pair of them had just come back from visiting Aunt Constance Oliver.

Isobel said, 'It's just as well we didn't know, it would only have upset her.'

Ethel dismissed the idea. 'She's gone beyond being upset by anything; half the time she didn't know we were there and once she asked me who I was.' Ethel drew her shawl more closely about her shoulders.

'Are you all right, mamma?'

'Of course I'm all right! You don't have to worry about me, but I think I'll go up to my room and lie down for a while.'

Nancy said, 'I'll come up in a few minutes and settle you in. Don't forget to switch on your fire.'

The old lady was irritated. 'For goodness sake, Nancy, don't fuss me! I'm perfectly capable of looking after myself. I shall be in my room if I'm wanted.'

Isobel said, 'I wish Henry would come back. It's awful not *knowing*.'

Celia said, 'If you remember, we were saying at lunch time that we'd none of us seen her all day. She could have been up there since last night . . .' She added after a moment, 'I wish Alice and the others were back, it's come over quite black.'

Isobel lit one of her eternal cigarettes and turned to Nancy, 'Did you know that she was using the tower for her tricks?'

'Yes, John said that she had some of her stuff stored on the top floor and that the roof was marked out with a star or something of the sort. Of course I had no idea she was going up there at night—if that is what she did.'

Large drops of rain appeared on the window panes and trickled down. Celia said, 'It's raining.' And suddenly the rain began to drive against the window in real earnest.

All three women were recalling a scorching June afternoon sixteen years before. Isobel remembered sitting on the beach where she had taken the twins to get them away from their mother who was rehearsing for one of her tantrums. She even recalled the book she was reading while the children played—Iris Murdoch's *Severed Head*. At that time Isobel had been making a study of contemporary women authors in the hope of discovering what they had that she lacked.

The twins were playing ducks and drakes with flat stones, then Laura had wandered off over the rocks. Isobel missed her and worried briefly but the child turned up all right though strangely excited. 'I saw mummy . . . I did! I saw mummy up the top of the tower . . . I saw her . . . I saw her . . .' She was tremulous with excitement and seemed desperately anxious to be believed. Then, abruptly, her face clouded, her eyes lost an almost wild look they had had and she went back to playing quietly with her brother.

Nancy remembered the breathless, pointless haste with which she had covered the distance from the tower to the house. Henry would not leave Deborah's body. On the way through the woods she had slipped and gashed her leg so that blood trickled down her shin and stained her sandals. When she reached the house it seemed to be deserted but she knew that there was a telephone in the library and she phoned Dr Fox from there.

'I was eighteen then,' she told herself. 'Eighteen . . .'

Celia remembered lolling on a chair-bed in the back yard where it was cool. She was playing with Alice who was a year and ten months old. She had come indoors, carrying the child, and over-heard Nancy telephoning in the library and sounding slightly hysterical. 'But she's dead, Dr Fox . . . She fell from the tower . . . She's dead . . .'

That evening too, the three of them had been together in the drawing-room while Ethel looked after the children and Henry talked to a policeman in the library.

Henry arrived at last, delivered by the police car, but soaked to the skin because they had had to run the gauntlet of the rain to get to the car. His khaki paint-stained denims dripped on the carpet and his thinning hair was plastered to his scalp. He told them what he knew in a flat voice for he had reached that stage of mental and physical exhaustion when he seemed to be no longer involved.

'There's not much I can tell you. It's Deborah over again . . . That damned tower!'

Isobel said, 'Are they bringing her home?'

They had carried Deborah down on a stretcher and Isobel had seen her lying on her bed, her arm twisted at an impossible angle and her whole body having a *crumpled* appearance.

'Oh, no. They think the coroner will order a post-mortem. Lobb said something about her having inhaled smoke from the herbs she was burning.'

'But what's that got to do with it?'

'Apparently the fumes could have made her giddy, like a drunken man rambling about. Then she could have fallen.' He broke off. 'Have you any idea when Harold will be back?'

Nancy guided him to the door. 'A drink, a hot bath and fresh clothes or you will be ill.'

Isobel and Celia were left alone. Isobel was standing at the window watching the rain sweep across the park. She shivered. 'I'm going upstairs to change into something warmer.' She was still wearing her blue chiffon.

Celia said, 'I wish Alice and the others would come; they must have known it was going to rain.'

Isobel went upstairs. With the gloom outside it was almost dark in the first floor corridor. She passed Henry's room, Nancy's and her own and came to Laura's with its door in the end wall. Laura's door was a little open, she pushed it wide and went in, closing it behind her. The room had a large window which faced out towards the plantation but the curtains were drawn and the light was so poor that objects in the room were only dimly visible. Isobel picked her way across to the window where there was a knee-hole desk and a chair—the only chair in the room. She would have liked to pull back the curtains but lacked the courage.

There was nothing on the desk but a lacquered box. Isobel lifted the lid and saw a miscellaneous collection of objects inside which meant nothing to her so she turned her attention to the drawers.

'I've got the right,' she told herself. 'Somebody has to do it and I'm her aunt.'

The bottom drawer was almost filled with duplicated reports of various societies concerned with occult and psychical studies; the top drawer held notepaper and envelopes, pencils, ball-points and a cardboard box of oddments such as rubber bands and paper clips. The middle drawer was locked. Isobel searched among the bits and pieces in the top drawer and found a small key which fitted the one which was locked. She opened it and started to go through the contents.

There were two hard-covered exercise books almost filled with writing in Laura's small, widely spaced script. One seemed to consist of notes on her reading in occult subjects; the other was a record of her own experiences and experiments. This one was heavily annotated in the margins. Isobel put them aside. Below them, resting on a pile of letters, was a book: *Sex, Marriage and Childbirth*. She turned her attention to the letters, several of which were still in their envelopes. There were letters from Lucille, from people with an interest in the occult, two or three from former school friends and it was one of these which caught and held Isobel's attention.

The letter began by expressing surprise at hearing from Laura after an interval of four years then went on, 'It seems that there was a philosophy tutor called Payne who left—'

'What are you looking for?'

Isobel let out a startled cry, badly shaken. It was her mother, who moved like a cat when she had a mind to.

'God! You frightened me, mother.'

'Did I?' The old lady did not seem in the least penitent. 'Pull back the curtains so that we can see what we are doing; this is like playing blind man's bluff.'

Isobel swished back the curtains with a clatter of wooden rings and the room came to grey life. Ethel looked round with interest. 'It's a long time since I was in this room. Your grandmother slept in here after grandfather died.' Her gaze travelled over the engravings, the Rose Cross, the floor-level mirrors and the profusion of cushions. 'I warned Henry before he married Deborah that the Olivers had a kink. It's come out again and again—always in the women. What were you looking for?'

Isobel swept the letters back into the drawer and replaced the books. She kept back the letter which referred to Payne. 'I thought she might have left a note.'

Ethel nodded. 'You're thinking the same as I am, that she probably killed herself. You can depend on it, if she did, then she left a note; she wasn't the sort to go without an explanation. But if she did leave something she wouldn't have hidden it away in a drawer.'

Isobel got up from the chair. 'Anyway, there's nothing here.'

Her mother walked away and stood looking at an enlarged version of one of Levi's engravings which was pinned to the wall. 'Of course, she might have sent it by post.'

'Sent what?'

'A note. Some suicides do; I suppose they do it to make sure that the right person sees it. Or she could have written direct to the coroner, I wouldn't put that past her. We shall know in the morning.'

They moved towards the door and Ethel removed the key from inside and inserted it outside.

'What are you doing?'

'I'm locking this door, it's better that way.'

'Any of the keys from the other rooms will fit.'

Isobel went to her own room and changed into a woolly jumper and slacks. She ran a comb through her hair and thought, The children will be back. The twins and Alice and John were still 'the children'. Isobel shut the door of her room behind her.

Nancy and Celia were in the drawing-room with John. They had made coffee and sandwiches and wheeled it in on a trolley. They had brought in a portable electric fire and there was an air of false cosiness.

'Where are the others?'

'Alice is with Harold and I think Henry is with them.'

John asked his mother, 'Did Laura kill herself?'

Nancy said, 'They think it might have been an accident, but we don't know.'

Henry came in looking vague and distressed. 'He doesn't want me.'

133

Isobel asked, 'How's he taking it?'

Henry had changed into slacks and a cardigan and they seemed to hang off him as though, absurdly, he had shrunk. He looked at his sister before replying. 'Badly. For some reason he blames himself. He says it wouldn't have happened if it hadn't been for him. I must say, Alice is wonderful with him.'

Nancy handed him a strong cup of coffee. 'Drink this.'

Chapter Seven

THE THREE WOMEN were subdued; it was still raining and the light was on in the kitchen, a single naked bulb which caused the shabby paintwork to gleam with yellow reflections. The wall-clock showed fifteen minutes to nine.

Celia was pale and almost haggard. 'Alice was with him until nearly two. I could hear him sobbing part of the time. It's not right, but what's the good of me talking? She takes no notice of what I say any more. And it's her birthday today. What can I say to her? I can't even wish her Many Happy Returns.'

Nancy said, 'Eighteen; it hardly seems possible. I was eighteen when Deborah died but Alice seems younger somehow.'

Isobel had not dressed; she was wearing an old quilted dressing-gown and she had not done her hair so that she looked like a blonde golliwog. Her features seemed to have lost something of their definition and there was a vague look in her eyes. She lit one cigarette from another.

Nancy said, 'Ethel seems to be taking it better than any of us.'

Celia shrugged. 'Ethel never did upset herself about other people's troubles.'

Nancy glanced up at the clock. 'I keep expecting her to come in . . . Somebody ought to let her partner know.'

Isobel said, 'She must have her own key.'

'All the same, she should be told.'

Celia pushed back her chair. 'I'll make some fresh coffee.' She switched on the electric kettle. 'I wonder what will happen to everything now.'

Isobel said, 'If you mean, what will happen to Laura's half of

Lucille's money then it depends on whether she made a will. If she did, it will go to Harold; if she didn't, then God knows.'

Nancy filled a cup with freshly made coffee. 'I'll take this to Henry. He's up there in his studio and he's hardly spoken a word since last night.'

As Nancy went out Alice came in wearing a cardigan over her nightdress. Her eyes were puffy with tiredness and she looked very young. 'I'll take up some coffee to Harold; he's awake. I don't think he slept at all.'

Celia said, 'I hope you'll put some clothes on.'

Her daughter ignored her.

Isobel said, 'I hope you have many happier birthdays, Alice. I know you will.'

'Thanks.'

Celia wondered why she couldn't have said that.

Nancy came back from the studio. 'He's very shaken. He's been on the telephone to the police and they're going to send someone out later to let him know how things stand—about the inquest and so on. They're doing a post-mortem.'

Miss Pearl arrived with the post, letting down her umbrella as she backed into the kitchen; she was agitated, like a bird with ruffled feathers.

'I really don't know what to say! Captain Holiday and I are most distressed! What a terrible tragedy for the family!'

As she spoke she sorted the mail. 'There are two communications for Sir Henry from Paris; nothing for Miss Isobel today; four for Lady Care . . .'

Isobel looked over the letters and glanced across at Nancy. 'Nothing there.'

'Were you expecting something?'

Isobel shook her head.

At ten-thirty a policeman and a policewoman arrived and spent half-an-hour with Henry and Nancy in the studio. Afterwards Nancy found Isobel still in the kitchen with Celia.

'The pathologist says she died from multiple injuries resulting from the fall but he also says that she must have inhaled a good deal of the smoke from burning herbs which would have made her dizzy so that she hardly knew what she was doing.'

Isobel said, 'It was no accident; you know it, we all know it. From what Henry said last night she must have fallen from the same spot as Deborah. What kind of accident is that?'

Nancy sat down as though overcome by weariness. 'No, I agree—'

'What puzzles me is that there is no note. I would have expected her to leave a note.'

'So would I. Is that why you were looking over the post just now? It never occurred to me. Perhaps we should look in her room.'

'Mother and I looked last night.'

'I see.' Nancy ran her fingers through her thick black hair. 'But there's something else they've come up with: Laura was pregnant.'

'*Pregnant*? How long?'

'A few weeks, apparently.'

'Good God!'

Celia said, 'That's the last thing I would have expected.'

There was silence in the kitchen for a long time, broken only by the hurried ticking of the clock and a dripping tap.

Isobel said, 'Did they have to open her to find that out?'

Nancy showed distaste. 'Certainly not! They can tell after a few weeks but in any case it seems that she had been to Dr Lobb for a pregnancy test. The test was positive and she had the result on Friday morning. Of course, Lobb told the pathologist.'

'I didn't know she went to Lobb, I thought she was with Fox like the rest of us.'

'Yes, well, it seems there were a lot of things we didn't know about her.'

'Did Lobb say whether she intended to have the baby?'

'Henry phoned him and he said Laura seemed delighted with the result of the test. She asked him for advice about how to behave, what to eat and so on.'

Isobel remembered the book on sex and marriage she had found in Laura's desk but she did not mention it.

Celia said, 'When you're pregnant, and especially with no

137

husband, you go through all sorts of queer phases. I should know, but I wouldn't have thought she was the sort to commit suicide, she liked herself too much, but I suppose she must have done. Anyway, people will say that she did. It's Deborah over again, it's where we came in. You'd almost think she planned it.'

Nancy said, 'For God's sake don't talk like that, Celia!'

Isobel said, 'Have the police gone?'

'No, they are still with Henry; they want to take a look at her room.'

'Why?'

'I don't know, perhaps they think they may find a note or something.'

Nancy thought, Only Henry and Harold are really grieving and with Henry it's largely a feeling of guilt, perhaps with Harold too.

Henry came in, looking ten years older, the colour had drained from his cheeks leaving a pattern of minute blood vessels like fine threads of saffron.

Isobel said, 'Have they gone?'

'No. They've found the ammunition belonging to Payne's gun.'

'Where?' Isobel was startled.

'In a lacquered box on her desk with a lot of oddments in it. It was at the bottom of the box, still in its cardboard container.'

'Is it all there?'

Henry said irritably, 'How do I know?' Then he added, more calmly, 'Unless Payne knows how many rounds there were there's no way of finding out.'

'They didn't find the gun?'

'No, but they are still looking.' He stood by the door, fiddling with his beard, not knowing whether to go or stay. 'Poor child! She must have thought of using the gun, then changed her mind . . .' He broke off to follow another line of thought, 'Those other things in the box, each with a date label tied to it—brooches and things— I didn't know what they were but I could see that the young policewoman thought it a bit odd. I don't suppose any of you . . .'

The three women denied any knowledge of the contents of the box.

They had lunch in the kitchen as usual, though Ethel was keeping to her room and Alice had joined John at the nurseries. Henry and Harold were there. Harold looked pale but composed. He felt empty—drained, but unnaturally calm, as though under sedation. Isobel thought that she detected a change in him, a change over and beyond the consequence of his present grief; for the first time she was seeing him as a man.

They sat round the table, Henry facing his son. Mostly they kept their eyes lowered but several times Nancy saw Henry looking at Harold with a slightly puzzled expression as though trying to take his new measure. No-one was hungry but they all felt it safer to follow the routine.

Harold could not have said what he was thinking, perhaps he was not thinking at all. He was aware of his father watching him.

After clearing his throat a couple of times Henry spoke, 'Did Laura tell you that she was pregnant, Harold?'

Harold felt the colour rising in his cheeks. Why did the question make him feel guilty? 'No, but on the day of Aunt Lucille's funeral she told me that she intended to have a child.'

'Did she say anything about marriage?'

'Only that she had no intention of getting married.'

Henry crumbled a bread-roll on his plate then seemed surprised by what he had done. 'Lobb says she seemed pleased that she was pregnant; it doesn't make sense to me.'

The clock on the wall ticked away another two or three minutes and Harold was wondering how soon he could leave the table without causing comment. Suddenly it had become necessary to consider one's every action. He had a strange feeling that the future—he supposed that he meant the future of the family—had become a fragile thing which could be shattered by an ill-considered word or an untimely act.

His father cleared his throat preparatory to another question which came, tentative and diffident, 'I don't suppose she mentioned the gun to you?'

'No.'

Another silence, then Celia said, 'If she had the ammunition she must have had the gun, but what did she do with it?'

The question hung in the air and Harold hoped that no-one would attempt to answer it but after an interval Isobel said, 'You remember what she said that night at dinner, about something missing from her room but she wouldn't say what—'

Henry cut in on his sister, alarmed and shocked, 'You're not suggesting that she was referring to the gun then?'

'Now that we know she had the ammunition it seems very likely.'

'But that would mean that somebody else—'

Harold could stand it no longer; he got up abruptly, upsetting his chair. 'Do you have to go on, and on, and on . . . ?' They were staring at him, as though transfixed. He felt foolish. He righted his chair and apologized. 'I'm sorry, I shouldn't have said that.'

They were sympathetic but he did not want sympathy. He turned to his father. 'I'm going into town this afternoon which means that I shan't be in the office—is that all right?'

His father said, hastily, 'My dear boy! Don't worry about the office!'

Harold felt that he must do something or be overwhelmed by guilt. Guilt for what? He scarcely knew. He went up to his room to fetch his jacket and as he passed his grandmother's room she called him.

'Harold! Come here, I want to talk to you.'

The old lady was seated at her table by the window engaged on one of her immense jig-saws. The cat was asleep on the window ledge. She looked up at Harold with her blue-grey eyes that could be almost hypnotic. As a child he had always dreaded being cross-examined by grandmother and he felt very little different now.

She said, 'You are going through a bad patch and I don't want to make things worse for you but there's something I've got to know.'

He stood, waiting.

'I've known for years about that lacquered box. I found out about it more or less by chance and I had a strong word with your sister and put a stop to it. You know what I'm talking about?'

'Yes.'

'Good! Well, that was nearly ten years ago but now the police have found the missing ammunition in that same box with all the other rubbish. I want you to tell me honestly whether the gun business was another of these stupid dares as she called them.'

He was so surprised that he forgot to be annoyed. 'Why, no! I knew nothing about the gun—'

She stopped him with a gesture, 'That's all I wanted to know. You can't blame me if I treat you like a child still. That's how you behave, but I can see signs that you're growing up.'

Laura's shop in Wharf Lane was next to an antique dealer in a street of rather off-beat establishments which included a cheese and wine bar, a rural craft shop, a patisserie and a Tao clinic. The Tarot Shop was painted sky-blue and the window was stacked with books, scrolls, birth signs in various forms and materials, the impedimenta of ritual magic, packs of tarot cards . . . A sign in the form of a tarot card—the Wheel of Fortune—hung like an inn board over the door. Through the window Harold could see a thin girl in a long cerise dress, serving a customer. She had a mop of curly brown hair and Harold remembered that Laura had introduced them on one occasion. Freda Price.

He waited for the customer to leave then pushed open the shop door. Wind bells tinkled and the thin girl came over.

'Oh, we've met before but in any case I would have recognized you; you're so much like your sister.'

She had a triangular face, freckled, with a real cupid's-bow mouth. 'I'm very upset about Laura. When they told me this morning on the phone I just couldn't believe it. I really can't take it in now; I've thought about nothing else all day.'

The shop smelled of incense, like a church.

'You're Freda, aren't you?'

'That's right—Freda Price.'

'Harold.'

He walked with her to the back of the shop where there was a curtained alcove with a desk, a couple of chairs and a filing cabinet, not to mention a sink and a gas-ring.

She ran her fingers through her tight brown curls and repeated, 'I can't take it in. What happened?'

Harold told her.

'You mean that she was conducting a summoning?'

'If that's what it's called. Did you know about it?'

The girl looked worried, 'I didn't know that she was going to try again.'

'Again?'

'We tried one Saturday a couple of months back.'

'At the tower?'

'Yes. I messed it up. Laura didn't say much at the time but I knew she was pretty mad. At the critical moment I started to cough.' She looked up at him with a tentative smile. 'When I start to cough it's like starting to laugh, I can't stop. It was the smoke from the brazier—those herbs she was burning, I couldn't help it. Of course it broke whatever spell there was . . .' After a moment she asked, 'Was there anybody with her this time?'

'No, she was alone.'

Freda nodded. 'You see! She wouldn't risk having somebody make a bish of it a second time.' She seemed to hesitate, then made up her mind. 'I don't know how you feel about all this . . .' She waved her hand vaguely to take in the contents of the shop and, by implication, the whole world of the occult. 'Personally, I can take it or leave it. I mean, it's interesting, you get a bit of a kick out of it, and it's a living, but for Laura it was different . . . She really *believed*; for her it was some kind of a religion and she was so *intense* . . .'

Freda was silent for a time then she said, 'God! I wish I hadn't balled it up the first time.'

Harold said, 'Whatever happened, it wasn't your fault. This summoning business—what was she trying to do?'

'She was trying to summon up a spirit—one of the Lords of Darkness, called Beelzebub, to answer her questions.' She stopped

142

with a sheepish smile. 'I suppose this all sounds daft to you but she made it convincing.'

'I know Laura.' Harold smiled an affectionate smile. 'But what questions? What did she want to ask about?'

'About her mother's death—about your mother's death.'

The wind-bells tinkled and Freda went to attend to a customer who bought a packet of joss-sticks and a censer to burn them in.

When she came back Harold said, 'Did you get on well together?'

She thought briefly. 'I suppose we must have done. Surprising, really; we weren't a bit alike but we hardly ever quarrelled in the eighteen months we were partners.'

'Did she tell you her troubles?'

'Such as?' The girl looked at him, mildly suspicious.

'Such as she was pregnant.'

'Really? No, she didn't tell me that though I'm not surprised.'

'You've no idea who the father was?'

'Not a clue! I know she was seeing some chap and she said she was having it off with him. I asked her if she was on the pill and she said she wasn't, that she wouldn't mind if she got pregnant. I didn't altogether believe her but she could have meant it.'

'And she didn't say anything more about this man that might help?'

'Precious little. All I can say is I got the impression he was an older man, but I could easily be wrong. She was always a bit mysterious about her private life and she changed the subject so often it was difficult to follow her anyway.'

Freda had two more customers, a pair of middle-aged ladies who deliberated over and finally bought a book on necromancy.

When they were gone Harold said, 'She went to the doctor on Friday morning and got the result of her pregnancy test.'

Freda looked surprised. 'Is that where she was? She told me she would be late and she turned up about eleven.'

'How did she seem? Depressed?'

'No. Just the opposite. Well, you know how she could be when things were going her way . . .'

Isobel and Cleo walked up through East Wood to Tresean. The rain had stopped and the skies had cleared but the trees still dripped and there was mud underfoot. It would have been easy to imagine that the past two months had never been; that she would find Tim in his workroom, that he would get up and come to her with that look of surprised welcome. 'Isobel!' They would talk books, he would suggest something that she might read, he would make tea then, a little later, they would go upstairs and lie together in the still, dimly-lit room which was like a cave.

But it was not going to be like that; she did not even want it to be. She was not going to Tresean with any hope or intention of renewing their relationship; on that she was quite clear. On the other hand she did not want to examine too closely her motives for going at all.

They walked up the drive together, Cleo and she, and crossed the patch of rough grass to the french windows. Sure enough they were open and the typewriter was clacking away. Cleo, slipping easily into former ways, went in; Isobel hung back.

'Isobel!' Certainly it was a greeting of surprise if not of welcome.

Isobel stood in the doorway; she said in a hard voice, 'I'm sorry to disturb you but you may not have heard the news . . .'

'You are not disturbing me, but what news?'

'About Laura.'

'What about her?'

'She is dead.'

'*Dead?*' His face which had been lively and responsive was suddenly a mask.

'So the police haven't been here yet?'

'The police? Why should—Oh, God! Not that damned gun?'

'No, not the gun. Laura's body was found late yesterday afternoon at the foot of the Prospect Tower. It seems that she must have fallen from the top.'

Payne said in a strained voice, 'What a terrible thing!' He went on after a moment, 'I heard cars in the lane yesterday afternoon around five but since the cottage has been let I've learned not to take any notice. When, exactly, did it happen?'

'Late on Saturday night or early on Sunday morning. She was carrying out some sort of ritual at the top of the tower—'

'Alone?'

'So it seems. The pathologist says that it's possible she was affected by the fumes from the herbs she was burning and that she became giddy and lost all sense of direction.'

'How awful! So it was an accident?'

Isobel hesitated. 'Possibly, according to the pathologist.'

'You seem doubtful.'

'She fell in exactly the same spot as her mother sixteen years ago. If it was an accident wouldn't that be a remarkable coincidence?'

Payne frowned. 'Yes, of course it would.'

Isobel said, 'Have you any idea what she was up to?'

He paused, and seemed to choose his words with care. 'I can only guess; she told me that she wanted to conduct a summoning—that is to say, she wanted to raise a spirit and put to it certain questions.'

'What questions?' Isobel's manner was becoming brusque.

'I don't know. I tried to dissuade her from anything of the kind—not because I thought that she would put herself in any physical danger but these rituals are highly emotive and they can have damaging psychological effects on sensitive or neurotic people.'

The glib phrases and the objective approach irritated Isobel; she found it difficult to understand why she had admired this capacity for calm, lucid exposition, along with his scholarship, his wry humour and his apparent intellectual and emotional self-sufficiency. Now she found herself resenting his book-lined room, his cushioned world, his ivory tower from which he allowed himself to descend from time to time to consort with ordinary mortals.

'Laura was pregnant.'

She saw him start.

The golden haired, green eyed maiden, permitted to lure the Romantic into her enchanted grove, has no right to become pregnant; she must remain the eternal virgin.

'Does that surprise you?'

He said, with obvious irritation, 'Of course it surprises me! Very much.'

'Didn't Bettina's friend, Caroline, kill herself beside the Rhine one night for the sake of a love affair gone sour?'

The grey, slightly protruding eyes looked startled. 'You are not suggesting that Laura killed herself because of me?'

'I don't know whether she did or not; all I can say is that I cannot believe that her death was accidental.'

He passed his hand over his forehead and across the mop of greying hair. 'Isobel! Is-o-bel!' He lingered over the syllables in a manner which gave them a sense of intimate appeal. 'You are hurting yourself as well as me.'

'Perhaps. In searching Laura's room, the police came across a cardboard box of ammunition.'

Again she saw the startled look in his eyes. 'But no gun?'

'No, they did not find the gun. Neither did they find this.' She took a folded sheet of notepaper from her pocket and dropped it on his desk in reach of his hand.

He did not touch the paper. 'What is it?'

'I found it when I was looking for a possible suicide note. I'll read it to you if you like.'

He said nothing and she picked up and unfolded the paper. 'It's a letter to Laura from a former school friend and after expressing surprise at hearing from Laura after an interval of four years, it goes on, "I made a few enquiries as you asked. It seems that there was a philosophy tutor called Payne who left under a cloud in either sixty-eight or sixty-nine. He was in the habit of taking girl students to bed with him and he got one of them pregnant. She lost her head and took an overdose. They didn't find her in time and so it was R.I.P. for the poor little cow. The parents, P's wife, and the senate, all took umbrage at this, so exit P. He must have had more of what it takes than most dons of my acquaintance for it seems that he left behind a whole gaggle of disappointed virgins who hadn't primed their little lamps in time . . ."'

Isobel stopped reading. 'I'll leave it with you.'

She walked out into the sunshine, leaving Cleo to follow sluggishly. Payne came to the door but did not call after her.

Isobel was surprised and excited by her own temerity. She thought, I used Laura against him—and why not? Why not, indeed? But as she became calmer she began to recall in more detail what had happened and she felt less pleased with herself. She said aloud, 'Do I really believe that Laura killed herself because of him?'

At six o'clock Alice was in her room. She had a book in her lap but she was not reading. It was one of those summer evenings, calm and still, which always reminded her of the saints in the hymn— 'casting down their golden crowns around the glassy sea'. If that was the best saints could look forward to . . .

Alice was thinking about her own future. To be or not to be. Lectures, practicals, tests, exams, notes, libraries, hostels, lodgings, students male and students female; to be free or frosty, to wear blue stockings or no pants, to pot or not to pot. Fab parties, hang-overs and hang-ups—or a virginal bed and *Gray's Anatomy*.

There is a middle way, but am I the sort to find it?

There was a tap at the door and Harold came in; she looked at him with concern and affection. 'You look better!' But she thought that he was alarmingly drawn and pale.

'How's the work at the nursery?'

'I've found muscles I didn't know I had and they all ache.' She pointed to the bed. 'Make yourself at home.'

He was strangely shy; self-conscious about the previous night when he had wept in her arms.

'Thanks for putting up with me last night. I'm afraid I made a complete fool of myself.'

Alice was gravely reassuring and unconsciously parental. 'Nonsense! You were in a state of shock and I was very worried about you. Are you sure that you are all right now?'

Harold went over to the window and stood with his back to her. 'I don't feel anything now.'

'Isn't that quite natural?'

'Is it?'

'It's the reaction.'

His voice sounded muffled. 'She was my sister, Alice—my *twin*. I used to think that if ever she was not around I wouldn't be able to go on . . . I don't mean that I needed to be with her all the time, just to know that she was . . . well, somewhere.'

Alice was too wise to point out that this was exactly what Laura had intended. She said, 'What have you been doing today?'

He turned to face her. 'That's the point, really. Yesterday I thought I'll find out how and why this happened if it's the last thing I do! I owe her that much, at least . . . Well, I went to her shop this afternoon and talked to the girl she worked with. Laura hadn't told her she was pregnant but she had talked about having sex with somebody.'

'Any idea who?'

'No, except that Freda had the impression it was probably an older man.' Harold spread his hands in a gesture of helplessness. 'Now I seem to have run out of steam; I don't know what to do next. It seems so *disloyal*.'

Alice went over to him and took his hands in hers. 'Don't torture yourself, Harold. What *can* you do?' She was looking at him, her eyes full of concern. Her hair curved round her cheeks and out again so that he had an almost hour-glass view of her face; her lips were parted and he could see the moisture glistening on her regular teeth. He thought, How beautiful she is! He said, 'The inquest is tomorrow.'

'Will you have to go?'

'I must.' He released her hands and turned away. 'I'm worried, Alice.'

'About the inquest?'

'In a way about the inquest but there's more to it than that.' Alice said nothing and he went on, 'The verdict tomorrow will be either accidental death or suicide, won't it?'

'Yes, I suppose so.'

He faced her with great seriousness. 'Laura didn't kill herself, Alice. I'm quite certain about that. She wanted to live. In her own way, which seemed odd to most people, she enjoyed life. She *wanted* to live. This baby—from what she told me I'm sure it wasn't a mistake, she told me that she intended to have a baby and she had all sorts of ideas about how she would bring it up.'

He looked at her with great intensity.

'I knew her, Alice, I understood her—at least better than anyone else did.'

She was puzzled by his insistence and she spoke gently. 'Isn't it most likely that they will bring in a verdict of accidental death? After all, it seems that the pathologist went out of his way to stress the effects of inhaling the smoke from those herbs.'

'Yes, I know. An accident. Perhaps they will say that as they said it about mother. Perhaps mother's death was an accident though nobody seems to believe it, but with Laura . . . Can you believe in the same accident happening in the same place—exactly the same place, twice? Laura fell from the same spot as mother . . .'

Alice was mystified. 'But if it wasn't an accident and she didn't—'

'If it wasn't an accident and she didn't kill herself then it was murder.' Harold swallowed hard and made an effort to control himself. 'I've no right to be unloading my worries on you like this but I can't keep it to myself any longer. You see, everybody is assuming that she was alone up there but we don't know that she was. Anybody could have been up there with her.'

'But who would want to kill Laura?'

Harold made a helpless gesture. 'I don't know but Laura seemed to go out of her way to upset people.'

'You don't kill somebody because they upset you.'

'No, but you might if they threatened you.'

'Threatened? Who could Laura threaten?'

Harold shook his head. 'You'll think I'm completely mad but it goes round and round in my head until I don't know what I believe or what I should do.' He went on in a more controlled voice, 'You must have heard that my mother was a very difficult woman to live with and that she drove father almost to desperation. Well, Laura believed that either father or Nancy pushed her off the tower.'

Alice was profoundly shocked. 'But that was a terrible thing to say! How could she possibly have thought of such a thing?'

'It seems that mother wrote to Aunt Lucille more than once saying in effect that she thought father might end up by killing her.'

'But that doesn't mean—'

'No, I know. I know. I was upset by what Laura said but I didn't believe it for a moment. When Laura disliked someone she could be very extreme. But can't you see that now the same thing has happened to her and recently she's been going around asking different people questions about exactly how mother died . . .'

Alice took his arm and they stood looking at each other. She was aware that he was reaching out to her like a man who prays. She was also dimly aware that if they were together in the future this would be the enduring pattern of their relationship. But that did not trouble her, she had no wish that it should be otherwise.

'I think you should do nothing.'

'But—'

'Listen! The inquest is tomorrow, the police have been here. If there is anything in what you have been saying, and I don't think there is, plenty of people will be asking questions and trying to get at the truth. At least wait until after the inquest. You should think how your father has been hit by all this, and how much more it would hurt him if he thought you were ready to believe such a thing of him with almost nothing to go on.'

The relief on his face was her reward.

Chapter Eight

ON TUESDAY MORNING the three women were in the kitchen as usual, eating toast and drinking coffee. The fly-blown face of the wall-clock showed five minutes to nine. It was a glorious morning, the sun had reached the stable block across the yard and the orange lichens glowed.

Harold came in from the yard.

Celia said, 'I thought you were still in bed.'

'I've been up since seven.'

'Do you want some toast?'

She cut off a round of bread. 'You can do it yourself but wait for the grill to warm up first. Have you seen your father?'

'He's down at the fish ponds raking out blanket weed. I suppose Alice has gone to the nursery?'

'She and John set off before eight.'

Harold thought, Laura is dead and the world doesn't stop. Everything goes on as before and I have to remind myself—*remind* myself that she is dead.

Nancy said, 'Henry wants me to go with him to the inquest and that means I shan't get across to the nursery this morning.'

Isobel looked across at her sister-in-law, 'I thought John looked a bit washed out this morning and he scarcely had a word to say for himself. He seems to have taken it all very hard.'

Nancy frowned. 'I know. He's so vulnerable; it worries me. I must try to have a word with him this afternoon but it's not easy to talk to him.'

Celia said, 'You should try talking to Alice.'

The kitchen door was open to the yard and they heard Miss Pearl's light step on the cobbles; there was a tap on the door and she came in with her bundle of mail.

151

'Good morning, Lady Care; good morning, everyone.' Miss Pearl's efficiency was manifest in the set of her head, the firmness of her jaw and the glint of the light on her gold-rimmed spectacles. 'A lot of post this morning!' She brushed back the crumbs on the plastic cloth and sorted her packages. 'Four for Sir Henry, three for Lady Care, five for Miss Isobel and one for Mr Harold. And there is a new jig-saw for her ladyship.' Miss Pearl always referred to Ethel, the dowager Lady Care, as 'her ladyship' to distinguish her from Nancy.

Isobel collected her mail, glancing over the other envelopes as she did so.

Harold's letter was from his father's solicitors. It was brief and to the point:

Dear Mr Care,

Estate of Lucille Constance Arnaud née Oliver, deceased
As executor of the above estate your father has appointed us to act on his behalf. He has kindly agreed to call at this office at 11 a.m. on Friday next and it would be most helpful if you could join him on this occasion.

Yours sincerely,
Arnold Wickett
for Bawden Wickett and Lamb

The three women watched him read, then fold his letter and put it in his pocket.

Nancy said, 'I'll get Ethel's tray.'

The routine of the house seemed to be carried along by its own momentum, two slices of bread-and-butter, a pot of tea, a jug of milk, a bowl for the cat . . .

'Good morning, mamma.'

The old lady was sitting up in bed as usual, her cat beside her. Nancy poured milk into the cat's bowl and it jumped down from the bed to drink it. Ethel nibbled away at one of her thin slices of bread-and-butter.

'Anything new this morning?'

'I don't think so. Harold had a letter from the lawyers.'

'What about?'

'I don't know; he didn't say.'

'Good for him! The boy is beginning to show some sense. They say that God moves in a mysterious way his wonders to perform—they're certainly right about that.'

Nancy looked at her mother-in-law with curiosity, 'What on earth do you mean by that?'

'Well, however upset we are about the way it came about, the fact remains that the future of Nanselow looks brighter now than it has done at any time since the war.'

'Mamma! How can you talk like that?'

'Because it's a fact. With Lucille's money and without his sister to talk him out of it Harold will probably be persuaded to bail us all out. In fact, from what I've seen lately I doubt if he's going to need much persuasion.'

Nancy shivered. 'Really, mamma, I don't like to hear you say such things. It sounds almost ghoulish.'

The old lady paused in the act of sipping her tea. 'Don't be hypocritical, child! Can you honestly say that such thoughts haven't entered your head since Sunday evening?'

Nancy was silent and Ethel went on, 'The inquest is this morning, isn't it?'

'At eleven o'clock.'

'They'll say that she committed suicide—bound to.'

'It could be a verdict of accidental death.'

'Not unless the coroner is a fool.' The old lady took her second piece of bread-and-butter. 'They gave Deborah the benefit of the doubt out of consideration for the family but you can't do that twice. "Suicide while the balance of her mind was disturbed."'

After a moment she went on, 'Can you believe that of Laura, Nancy?'

'I can't see any other explanation.'

Ethel sighed. 'No. But without a note. Who would have thought that Laura could kill herself without getting the last ounce of drama out of it? It wouldn't surprise me one bit if the coroner produced a note at the inquest, like a rabbit out of a hat . . . In fact, Nancy, I'd feel a lot easier in my mind if he did.'

'I don't understand what you are getting at mamma.'

Ethel was vague. 'No? Well, it doesn't matter what I think anyway.'

The coroner was one of those surprising men who despite the drawbacks of small stature and a high-pitched voice managed to be authoritative without being pompous. His manner was dry, precise and brisk.

'These proceedings are directed solely to ascertaining who the deceased was and how, when and where she came by her death. All else is irrelevant. I shall first take evidence of identification. Call Sir Henry Cross Care.'

The coroner sat at a table covered with a green cloth in front of the stage in the village hall. The hall was booked that night for a folk concert and there were rows of empty chairs. Sitting at the front, Nancy had Harold on one side and a young reporter chewing gum on the other.

'Take the book in your right hand and repeat after me, "I swear by Almighty God . . ."'

Henry gave his evidence in a calm and subdued manner.

'Thank you, Sir Henry; you may stand down but I shall recall you later to answer other questions.' The coroner glanced over his sparse audience. 'I call John Charles Curtis to testify to the finding of the body.'

The young man who, with his girl friend, had found Laura, took the stand.

'You are John Charles Curtis, garage mechanic?'

'Yes, sir.'

'Take the book . . .

'Call Dr John Lobb . . . You are a medical practitioner and on Sunday afternoon last at about four-thirty you were called . . .

'Call William Fouracre Dakin . . . You are a pathologist attached to the County Hospital? . . . On my instructions you

154

carried out a post-mortem examination of the deceased. Will you tell the Court what you found?'

The pathologist made a brief statement and answered a few questions.

'In your report, Dr Dakin, you mention having found evidence that the deceased had inhaled certain noxious fumes believed to have come from burning herbs, but you also made it clear that death was due to the fall and not to asphyxiation.'

'That is so, the fumes would have had no more than a mildly narcotic and, perhaps, hallucinatory effect.'

'Precisely.'

In a surprisingly short space of time Henry was on his feet again.

'I would remind you, Sir Henry, that you are still under oath. I am sorry at this time to have to recall an earlier tragedy in your family; I refer to the death of your first wife, sixteen years ago.'

The reporter stopped chewing for a moment and paid attention. Sixteen years ago he had probably been wearing plastic pants.

'Is it not the case, Sir Henry, that she died in circumstances almost identical with those which are the subject of this present inquiry?'

'Yes, it is.'

'I understand that the deceased recently marked the spot from which her mother fell with an inscription meticulously cut into the stonework.'

'That is so.'

'Would you say that her mother's death and the manner of it have been much in her mind in recent months?'

'That is certainly true.'

'And is it the case that her body was found in almost precisely the spot where her mother's fell sixteen years ago?'

'Yes.'

'Thank you, Sir Henry, you may stand down.'

The coroner summarized the evidence, he cleared his throat and went on, 'In all the circumstances I must conclude that the deceased took her own life at a time when she was under consider-able emotional stress. This stress arose in part from brooding on her mother's death which occurred at a most impressionable stage in her childhood, and it was aggravated by the recent death of a much-loved aunt in a road accident.

'I therefore record a verdict of suicide while the balance of her mind was disturbed and I extend to the bereaved family my deep sympathy in their most tragic loss.'

It was still short of half-past twelve when they found themselves out in the sunshine once more. The three of them got into Henry's car. A few of the villagers were at their doors and there were faces at some windows.

Nancy said, 'Well, it's over.'

Henry sighed. 'Yes, and the coroner was very considerate—very.'

They drove out of the village and turned off down the lane which led to Nanselow.

Nancy said, 'Drop me off at the nursery. I've no idea what's going on there. Tell Celia I shan't be in for lunch.'

Isobel doodled on her typewriter, the Muse had deserted her—gone away to live; temporarily, she hoped. In the circumstances the only thing to do was to type something, read it, and squirm. That meant that one still had a critical faculty and there was hope.

But there were other things on Isobel's mind: she was thinking about Laura. Harold had mentioned an older man. Payne? Who else? To Isobel it seemed obvious. Did that mean that Payne had fathered the child who died with its mother? More than likely. If Laura really had been shopping round for an eligible male she could hardly have chosen better. Payne was highly intelligent, he had satisfactory looks, good health, and a share of that indefinable attribute—breeding—which, if it meant anything, must surely figure in the genetic hand-out from such a man.

But how had she gone about it? Being Laura, certainly not by making Payne a straightforward proposition. The situation would have been so complicated, dramatized and embroidered that the man would never know whether he had made a conquest or been raped. And here, the letter which Isobel herself had shown him

156

might be significant. Laura had searched out his seamy past. Had she used some sort of blackmail? In some ways Payne was an innocent; even Isobel realized that. Only innocents are lured and beguiled by the maidenhead.

So far her thoughts had drifted, then she realized with a shock where they had led her. She had visualized a highly emotional relationship between Payne and Laura with potentially explosive ingredients. Imagination? Not entirely. Most relationships with Laura were potentially explosive and a sexual one would not be an exception.

Then a fragment of her last conversation with Payne came back to her.

Isobel: 'She was carrying out some sort of ritual at the top of the tower—'

Payne: 'Alone?'

Isobel: 'Apparently.'

And later Payne had said, 'She told me that she wanted to conduct a summoning . . .'

It was from Payne that Laura had borrowed books on occult subjects. What was more likely than that she had discussed her plans with him?

Isobel tried to dismiss the idea but it would not go away; it had the tenacity of a good plot for a book, it possessed her.

Nobody had believed that Laura's death was an accident and so they had decided that she must have killed herself. Although those who knew her best found suicide difficult to accept, what was the alternative? There wasn't one because everyone had assumed that Laura was alone at the tower. But that was no more than an assumption, there was no evidence to support it; in fact, what evidence there was pointed the other way—on the only other occasion they knew about she had employed an assistant.

No-one had considered the possibility of murder.

Isobel shivered. What am I saying? Am I thinking this simply because . . . She laughed without seeing any joke. A woman scorned—that's me!

*

The funeral was on Thursday afternoon. Laura was to be buried in her mother's grave, a position originally reserved for Henry who had since decided on cremation. The little church was full and people lined the paths in the churchyard. Henry and Nancy walked behind the coffin followed by Harold and Isobel, Celia and John, Alice and Freda, with Wickett, the lawyer, bringing up the rear, silver haired and statuesque in his dignity.

It was hot; the sexton had been mowing the grass and the air was filled with its tantalizing fragrance. They gathered at the graveside and the vicar read from the Service for the Burial of the Dead, 'Man that is born of a woman . . .'

Alice wore her school skirt which was grey and a grey silk blouse she had borrowed from her grandmother. Opposite her, on the other side of the grave, Henry and Nancy stood together, familiar yet strange in their sombre clothes. Laura had accused one or other of them of murder and Harold was troubled because he could not believe that his sister had taken her own life. But to imagine that either of them had been concerned in her death was fantastic. They were ordinary, kindly people; they had been good to her mother and to her . . .

But do murderers look or behave differently from other people? Are they recognizable—not as murderers—but as being in some way abnormal? Did my father look like a manic-depressive when he was doing his accountancy or taking mother out to lunch? Was there something about him to suggest that one day, soon, he would hang himself in the lavatory of a lunatic asylum? Do I look as though I have a statistical predisposition to go the same way?

Harold was standing next to her at the graveside; he was conscious of her proximity and felt guilty because of it. Surely at such a time he should have thoughts only for his sister? He thought, I am despicably shallow. Out of the corner of his eye he could see Alice's profile; her expression was sad and compassionate. Compassion, that was the word; if only people were more compassionate. His sister's coffin was being lowered into the open grave.

'Forasmuch as it has pleased Almighty God of his great mercy to take unto himself the soul of our dear sister . . .'

They were throwing crumbs of black soil on to the coffin, down into the pit. It was barbaric. He tried to feel distress, grief, pity, but he would feel no more than a vague sense of oppression.

Celia was wearing the grey knitted frock she usually kept for Mass. She was very pale and there was a blotchy redness about her eyes. Onlookers probably thought that she had been weeping for the dead girl. Her lips moved mechanically, 'Holy Mary, mother of God, pray for us sinners, now and at the hour of our death . . . now and at the hour of our death . . .'

Nancy was watching her son. John stood, pale-faced, almost at attention, his eyes unfocused, his face closed. She had tried to talk to him but without success; he was polite, as always, but she could find no way to penetrate his reserve. She thought, This is the first time anyone close to him has died. Death has become something more than a distant threat, a shadow on the years ahead . . . Then, for no obvious reason, Ethel's words recurred to her mind, 'God moves in a mysterious way . . . If only Harold could be persuaded . . .' Nancy shivered.

Isobel was wearing a tweedy two-piece because it was the most sombre item in her wardrobe but the sun was blazing down and she could feel the sweat on her forehead and between her shoulder blades. She knew that she was flushed and she felt giddy. Surreptitiously she moved back from the edge of the grave and stood with her feet planted firmly apart.

Henry looked down at his daughter's coffin and saw a little golden-haired girl who stood between his knees and reached up with tiny exquisite fingers to touch his moustache.

'From henceforth blessed are the dead that die in the Lord.'

They returned to the house in the hired cars. Celia was restless, she could not bear the thought of going into the house, to the ritual of light refreshment and drinks for the few who had returned with the family mourners.

'To hell with them! Let them find out what it's like to do without me for once.'

She found herself walking across the park in the direction of East

159

Wood where she had not been for years. She climbed the path through the woods, skirted the top of the promontory where the tower was, and continued down the steep slope to the lane. She decided that she would make a complete circuit and return by way of the main drive. For two days she had been telling herself that she needed to think and for two nights her thoughts had chased each other round in circles.

Telling Alice about her father had brought it all back in a way she would scarcely have believed possible. All the old anguish was there, the unhealed wound, and in reaction she felt more than ever cheated and deprived of life. She had devoted herself to bringing up her daughter and her daughter had grown away from her. What now? I have no friends and few acquaintances, only a family with whom I live in a state of truce.

I am thirty-eight; perhaps not too old to start again.

She reached the bottom of the slope and turned up the lane. Piper's Cottage—another closed chapter. The windows of the cottage were wide open to the sun, sashes meeting. A woman's voice called to someone inside the house; a girl in a minimal bikini, sunbathing in the garden, eyed her with a certain critical disdain— or so she thought. She cringed inwardly as she often did when scrutinized by a stranger.

Henry insisted on calling the people in the cottage, 'Nancy's lodgers'. A family on holiday. Celia had never been on a family holiday in her life and on few holidays of any sort.

In the hedgerows there were blackberries and swelling sloes, honeysuckle and meadowsweet, fleabane and hemp agrimony. Autumn was just around the corner. Celia thought, I live in a beautiful place but most of the time I don't even see it. She walked on, mulling over problems which she could not possibly solve because she had not decided exactly what they were.

She thought, I don't know how to live; I have never known. I behave as though this were some sort of rehearsal, a time to learn, but it is the real thing—all I am going to get. I must believe in a future which will be better; otherwise I might as well put an end to it. Like Laura.

Had Laura lost faith in her future? Nobody would have thought so. If what she had said to Harold and to the doctor could be believed, even the baby was a declaration of faith. Yet Laura was dead.

'Good afternoon, Mrs Gilbert.'

Payne, leaning on his gate.

'I thought you would have been at the funeral.'

'I have; it's over.'

'I hardly knew whether to go or not and I decided on balance that it was probably better not to.'

Celia said nothing but she lingered, reluctant to break this thread of human contact.

He said, 'Isn't it strange that we have been neighbours for all these years and we've only spoken a few times?'

'Yes, I suppose it is.'

'You are out for a walk?'

For some reason the question struck her as slightly absurd and she smiled, a weary little smile which, nevertheless, brought her face to life, a complete change from that absent, almost vacant look which had become characteristic of her features in repose.

'Yes, killing time really.'

He smiled too, and his prominent grey eyes twinkled. 'Like the Mad Hatter.'

'Oh?'

'Wasn't he accused of murdering time?'

She laughed outright. 'Yes, of course! in *Alice*.'

'Mandatory reading for any pretending philosopher. Anyway, I am just about to make a cup of tea; I don't suppose you would care to join me so that we can kill him together?'

'Thank you. That sounds pleasant.' She had almost forgotten how to be agreeable to people and she had to cast about for the polite responses which seemed to come to others so naturally.

She walked with him up the drive, across the grass and into his room. 'What a lovely room!'

'You think so?' He seemed pleased.

Something about the room appealed to Celia, it was sunlit, cool and airy but beyond all that it conveyed a sense of purpose, of order and of serenity. She looked with satisfaction at the lines of books and up at the pictures.

She did not know what to say so she said, 'You are a philosopher, I think.'

He smiled. 'Of a sort.'

'I'm afraid I know nothing about that sort of thing; in fact I'm rather a stupid person.'

'Stupid? I'm quite sure that you are not! You may or may not know much about philosophy but I have rarely seen a more intelligent face—especially when you smile. If I might make a guess I'd say that you don't often smile—you should.'

Celia felt her colour rising and turned away.

Payne was contrite. 'You must forgive me, that was a most insensitive remark in the circumstances.'

Celia said, 'Not at all! It wasn't that. Naturally I'm very sorry about what happened to Laura but I can't pretend to be deeply grieved. We have never been very close—not at any rate since she was a small child. In fact, I don't think Laura was close to anybody except, perhaps, her brother.'

She thought, I am talking too much.

Payne gathered up the books from his desk and replaced them on the shelves.

'Laura was a very remarkable young woman.' He moved to the door. 'Do make yourself at home while I get the tea. By the way, which do you prefer, China or Indian?'

'China would be nice.'

A little later when they were sipping China tea and nibbling biscuits, Celia said, 'You know that the police found the ammunition belonging to your gun?'

'Yes, among Laura's things.'

'Do you think it was she who took it?'

Payne's grey eyes rested on hers for a moment before he answered, 'I think so.' After a moment or two he said, 'Do you mind if I ask you a question?'

'Of course not.'

'Who was it who told the family about my gun—Isobel, or Laura?'

'Laura—why?'

He smiled. 'I wondered.'

'You knew her quite well, didn't you?'

Payne replied carefully. 'She came here fairly often to refer to my mother's books and we talked a lot.'

'Did she strike you as the kind of person who might commit suicide?'

The practised pause of the professional teacher. 'Is there such a *kind* of person? I don't know. Aside from depressives and schizophrenics it seems doubtful whether there is a particular group of people with an inherent predisposition to suicide. Durkheim's theory—' He broke off with a disarming smile, 'But that's another story. My impression is that Laura was far too committed to life to want to leave it. There were so many experiences she wanted to have and so many things she wanted to do—particularly in connection with her interest in the occult. After all, at the time of her death it seems that she was engaged in an experiment which was important to her.'

Payne held out the plate of biscuits. 'Do help yourself to biscuits; the coconut ones are rather nice.' He studied the plate himself and selected one with deliberation.

Celia said, 'I know nothing about the occult but is it remotely possible that she died as a direct result of her experiment? What was she trying to do?'

The faintest trace of a smile played about Payne's lips. 'She was trying to raise a demon. To be frank, I think that the only demons one is likely to raise are from within one's self and in Laura's case I don't think they would have been self-destructive.'

'But her death couldn't have been an accident, could it? I mean, that would be stretching coincidence too far, don't you think?'

'Yes, I do. The close similarities between her own death and that of her mother certainly point to suicide—and suicide as a consequence of an obsessional concern with the way her mother died. I know that she was concerned but not, I think, obsessed.'

Celia's acquaintance with academics and their little ways was slender and she was deeply impressed by Payne's wide-ranging knowledge, the authority of his statements and the lucidity of his expression. She was a little too naïve to realize that he was responding to her obvious admiration, that he had expanded like a flower in the sun, and said more than he had meant to.

'Will you have a little more tea? It's still quite hot.'

Celia said, demurely, that she had had enough though she would have liked more.

Payne sat back in his chair, his relaxed tutorial manner taking charge. 'Of course the idea is absurd but if it were remotely feasible that Laura had been murdered then it would be comparatively simple to construct a theory to fit the facts.'

'Murdered!'

Payne made a dismissive gesture. 'I'm sorry. I've no business to theorize over such a tragic occurrence.'

'Please!' Celia was intrigued and flatteringly persuasive.

Payne gave in gracefully. 'It's simply that the circumstances of a summoning would have made it comparatively easy for anyone who wished harm to Laura. It would not have been difficult, I think, to bring about her death and make it appear as suicide.'

'How?'

Payne hesitated, apparently to collect and collate his ideas. 'You have to imagine the atmosphere of the ritual and the state of mind of the summoner—the darkness, the top of the tower under the night sky, the fluttering candles, the clouds of incense, the often meaningless but deeply moving incantations and invocations . . .'

He smiled and recited dramatically, '"I conjure and command thee O Beelzebub, Lord of the Flies, by him who spoke and it was done, by the most Holy and Glorious Names Adonai, Elchim—" I forget the rest but it goes on, "Show thyself to me here, outside this circle in fair and human shape, without horror or deformity and without delay . . . Come at once, visibly and pleasantly, and do what I desire . . ." That's all I can remember.'

'Is that what Laura would have recited?'

'Something like it and a great deal more of the same sort. But you notice the emphasis on the demon appearing in fair and

164

human shape? In the records of allegedly successful summonings the demon has often appeared in the form of a friend, a wife or a mistress; perhaps a near relative. By this stage in the proceedings the summoner is far gone in a trance-like state, partly self-induced, partly a result of inhaling the smoke from narcotic herbs . . .' He broke off and looked at Celia. 'You see the possibilities of such a situation?'

Celia was shaken. 'Indeed I do!'

Payne shrugged. 'But all this is nonsense, of course. Who would want to harm Laura?'

They talked a little longer and of other things but Celia could not free her mind of the image Payne had placed there. She could see Laura standing alone on the top of the tower, in the middle of her magic circle, lit only by the candle flames. And this other . . .

In the end she stood up to go.

'So soon?'

'I have to get an evening meal for the family.'

'Yes, of course.'

He walked with her to the gate. 'I hope that you will come again—come whenever you are passing this way. I shall look forward to it.'

On Friday morning Harold went with his father to keep their appointment with the lawyer. Harold drove the old Rover but he could find no room in any of the car-parks and had to leave it in a side street a long way from the town centre. They were ten minutes late for their appointment.

Wickett was old, mild-mannered and loquacious but reputedly shrewd. 'Always a pleasure, Sir Henry . . . Harold . . .' Harold grasped the lawyer's hand which was as soft as a girl's.

His father and the lawyer talked and from time to time he was included by way of parenthesis: 'You see, Harold, the estate has to be administered under French law . . .'

He listened politely.

It was difficult to believe that they were talking about things which intimately concerned him. He knew that he was to inherit

165

half his aunt's estate and he had thought seriously about how he might use the money to do something for Nanselow, but it was hardly more real to him now than on that evening, six or seven years earlier, when Lucille had said, 'I've made my will, children! Everything I have will be yours one day.'

The lawyer's office, his dry manner, his gentle, monotonous, sawing voice had little obvious connection with the luxurious Paris flat and the affection with which Lucille tried to smother them.

Wickett was undoing the tape on a thin pocket file. He drew out a single sheet of paper and laid it on his desk, reading it through, as though seeing it for the first time.

Without looking up, he said, 'When your sister, with another young woman, agreed to set up the business in Wharf Lane, we prepared the deed of partnership, and at the same time we were instructed to draw up her will. This is it. Under its provisions you are appointed as her sole executor and trustee and you inherit all her property.'

Wickett looked over his glasses at Harold. 'When she made this will your sister had little more to leave than her interest in the Wharf Lane shop and a small annuity from her mother's estate; now, of course, there is her inheritance under your aunt's will.'

The lawyer clearly expected him to be impressed but the sheet of paper on the desk seemed to have little more to do with him than the thousands of others in the files. His first reaction was one of astonishment that, almost two years earlier, Laura had made a will! It was fantastic; he could not imagine her thinking of such a thing.

But Wickett's voice sawed remorselessly on like a stridulating grasshopper, 'So that now you will inherit the whole of your aunt's estate after the complicated business of duty on both wills has been settled.'

Harold was intensely surprised; he had not thought about what would happen to Laura's share, and if he had, he would have assumed that it would go to his father.

But the lawyer gave him no pause. 'The proximity of the two deaths might give us grounds to ask for an abatement of duty, but there is the problem that in one case we have to operate under French law . . .'

A few weeks earlier Harold would have closed his mind at this point, distressed by the fact that the deaths of his sister and his aunt should become the subject of a legal and business wrangle, but time spent under the tutelage of Captain Holiday had gone some way to change that. He now knew that the management of a family estate must be concerned with such things as rents, mortgages, taxation, interest rates and capital investment, but surpassing all these in importance is the normal cycle of birth and death—especially death, for an inopportune death can transform a tax collector into a bailiff overnight.

So Harold listened to the lawyer and tried to learn but he was glad when they could escape into Lemon Street with its constant stream of traffic and people always hurrying to be somewhere where they were not.

When they were in the car his father said, 'I think you find all this business of wills and estate duty and so on, a bit sordid when it concerns people you loved.'

Sordid was not the word he would have chosen but he let it stand.

They had already turned off down the ferry road before either of them spoke again, then Harold said, 'I can't believe that Laura killed herself.'

His father said nothing for so long that when he eventually spoke Harold did not at first realize that it was in answer to his remark. The car was turning into the drive when Henry said, 'I felt exactly the same about your mother, Harold. It seemed incredible to me that anyone so vital—so aggressively alive, should take her own life in a moment of . . . of *wildness*.'

The car slowed to pass over a cattle-grid.

'For that is what happened, Harold, whatever the coroner said about accidental death. I've never spoken of this to you before or to anyone . . . Your mother was an exceptional woman, beautiful, talented, vivacious . . . But she lived in a state of continual tension, like a tightly coiled spring. She did everything to excess—loving, hating, giving, taking, laughing, crying . . .

'Living with her was like trying to keep one's balance on a high wire—all the time.'

Henry turned and glanced at his son. 'In many ways Laura was like her but Laura was more restrained; perhaps with Laura there was more head and less heart—I don't know. Deborah's reactions were almost always explosive; with Laura there was more calculation. But neither of them could tolerate the norms of life.'

Henry turned the car into the yard and drove into the old coach house. He cut the engine but made no move to get out.

'Do you understand what I am trying to say?'

'I think so.'

'You knew Laura better than I did and you must have realized that in a certain mood—a certain state of excitement or elation, she was like her mother—totally unpredictable and capable of anything.'

The light was dim in the coach house but Harold was aware of his father's gaze, intense and searching. He said, 'Yes, I think I know what you mean.'

Henry sighed. 'They were neither of them easy people to live with, Harold, but I am certain that most of all, they found it difficult to live with themselves.' After a moment or two he added, 'They'll be having lunch, let's go and join them.'

Harold knew that he had been offered a formula. Did it approximate to the truth? It must do; it had to do. There was no conceivable alternative.

Chapter Nine

SATURDAY MORNING. A soft warm morning with thin high cloud which would disperse as the sun grew stronger. Alice and Harold were in the kitchen with the three women. Alice wore bib-and-brace overalls, slim and slick, for her work in the nursery. Isobel thought, She could look good in a coal sack.

Harold said, 'Are you working this afternoon?'

'No, John is; I'm off.'

'Shall we do something?'

Alice got up and put her cup, saucer and plate by the sink. 'If you like.' She reached the door. 'See you at lunch, then. 'Bye!'

A little later Harold said, 'I must be going or Miss Pearl will beat me to it.' He spoke diffidently, half humorously, as he always did about his job in the estate office; probably to anticipate possible sarcasm.

When he had gone Isobel said, 'The new workers.'

Nancy said, 'I shall miss Alice when she goes; she's very good. She's got a real feel for plants, not like some of them who treat the plants as though they were plastic and wire.'

Celia nibbled a piece of toast without relish. 'I don't know what she's doing about King's and I daren't ask. She was supposed to let them know when her results came out.'

The atmosphere in the kitchen had changed; the three women were circumspect, more formal. Conversation was even more banal than usual and there were long, self-conscious silences when the clock came into its own.

Isobel lit a cigarette and thought, We all look like the morning after but with no night before. Nancy has lost weight; the last few weeks have been a strain on all of us. Some day, perhaps, we shall see the brighter side. Maybe there is something in Henry's destiny theme after all. If so, it's rough on some.

Since her encounter with Payne, and despite her concern for Alice, Celia had been unable to rid herself of the preposterous notion that Laura had been murdered. From time to time she asked herself why it was preposterous and she could find only one answer which was really another question. If Laura was murdered, who killed her? Obviously, it was unthinkable.

Nancy said, 'I'll get Ethel's tray.' It was ten minutes to nine by the clock on the wall. Pot of tea, jug of milk, cup, saucer, plate, bowl for the cat . . .

'Good morning, mamma.'

Everything as usual. The old lady was sitting up in bed, stroking her cat. The table by the window was almost covered by a huge jig-saw nearing completion, a reproduction of a painting by Watteau.

Nancy said, 'You've nearly finished it, you must have been up half the night!'

Ethel snapped, 'Don't talk to me about it! All those damned greens!'

Nancy filled the cat's bowl, the cat jumped off the bed. Ethel folded one of her two thin slices of bread-and-butter and nibbled it.

Everything as usual except that Nancy was conscious of a change and the change was in Ethel. Ethel was watching her.

'What did you do with it, Nancy?'

Nancy froze. 'What did I do with what?'

The old lady made a derisory sound. 'With the gun. What did you do with the gun?'

Nancy shrugged. 'I don't know what on earth you're talking about, mamma.'

'Of course you do, child! I'm not a fool. I've seen you going into her room several times in the past couple of months and I've heard you in there. What's more I was watching you that evening when she came in and said she'd missed something from her room. It took you a long time to find, didn't it?'

'Really, mamma—'

'Don't start telling me stories, Nancy! I'm too old for that. You

170

knew as well as I did that it was Laura who took the thing from Payne's desk. Who else? Isobel? Isobel would have been scared to touch it. Dippy Saunders? Can you imagine that boy going into a civilized room, searching it and going off with the gun, leaving the place more or less as he found it? If Dippy Saunders had been there Payne would have thought a herd of young steers had trampled through.

'But Laura—Laura saw her chance to make a bit of trouble. First she told everybody about the gun, then she took it. You realized that quick enough but you also thought she might have the crazy idea of using it in some way. In any case it would be safer in your hands than hers. I'm not blaming you, Nancy, I'm only asking what you did with it?'

Nancy did not answer at once, then she said, 'I dropped it down the well.'

'Good! Best place for it. Was it loaded?'

'I've no idea; I know nothing about guns.'

Ethel was smiling. 'Now tell me where you found it.'

'That low table which is a bit like an altar, where she used to burn her joss-sticks. If you pull it out from the wall there's a drawer in the back. It's not easy to see; I nearly missed it.'

Ethel said, 'You certainly look after the family, Nancy. You've done well by Nanselow.'

It was an accolade. So might Richelieu have said, 'This woman deserves well of the State.'

Nancy was leaving but as she reached the door Ethel said, 'What's the matter with John? He seems very put out about something.'

Nancy paused, her hand on the door knob. 'I don't know, I'm a bit worried about him. Of course he's taken a couple of hard knocks in recent weeks. First, Alice made it obvious that she prefers Harold's company to his and second, there's Laura's death. He seems to have taken that very much to heart.'

'Have you talked to him?'

'I've tried.'

'I'll see what I can do.'

Nancy hesitated. 'I don't want him to feel that he's being got at.'

Ethel poured herself a second cup of tea. 'I'm not daft, Nancy. In my opinion there's more to this than grief for Laura or having his nose put out of joint by Harold.'

Harold said, 'Will you do something for me this afternoon?'

'What?'

'Come with me to the Prospect Tower to collect Laura's things. I've been putting it off and I don't fancy doing it alone.'

He got a warm smile.

'We could go swimming afterwards if you felt like it.'

The afternoon was hot. For once August was living up to an undeserved reputation and giving visitors a taste of real summer. The estuary was peppered with sails; pleasure boats from Falmouth cruised up river, and on the opposite bank a long line of cars waited for the ferry, their chromium glittering through the trees.

They climbed the stone steps of the tower. On the top floor there was a canvas bag lying in a corner but they continued to the roof. Rain and sun had bleached the bright colours of the wands, rust tarnished the blades of the little dagger and the sword, ash from the brazier was scattered over the lead.

Harold stood looking at the scene. It was the first time he had been up the tower since that Saturday when it had dawned on him that Alice was no longer just a little girl about the house.

Alice said, 'I'll get the bag.' She thought that he might want to be alone.

The police had shown little if any interest in the bag. It held one of Laura's winter coats, a frock, a pair of sandals and a torch. Alice shivered at the thought of undressing by the light of a pocket torch in that eerie place then going out on to the roof alone to conduct some weird ritual. It needed courage. But why go through all that to kill oneself?

Alice closed her mind to speculation; it could lead nowhere— nowhere at all. She carried the bag up the steps to the roof. Harold was still standing where she had left him and there were tears in his eyes and in his voice.

'Silly, isn't it? Silly and sad. That's how it strikes me now, but when I was with her I half believed.'

Alice squeezed his arm.

They gathered the things together and, with the exception of the little brazier, packed them into the canvas bag.

'That's it, then.'

They left the bag in the ground-floor room of the tower to collect on their way back from the quay where they were going to swim. They trudged down the slope to the lane and along a rutted cart track through one of Saunders's fields where his milking cows nuzzled hopefully among a crop of docks and thistles.

Harold said, 'If father could get rid of old Saunders we could put in somebody to run it and knock the place into shape. It's eighty acres of our best land.'

Alice laughed. 'You're hooked, aren't you?'

'I suppose I am, I wouldn't have believed it possible six months ago.'

The quay was close to the ferry and passengers on the ferry watched the slim golden-haired young man and the dark, handsome girl. No doubt they thought, There, surely, must be happiness.

They swam and played and raced and dived until they were tired and afterwards, when they were sitting on the edge of the quay with their legs dangling, Harold said in a voice which sounded strangled, 'We could get married. There's nothing to stop us now.'

'There is—me.'

'Won't you marry me, Alice?'

'No.'

'Never?'

'Never is a long time and I doubt if you would wait that long.'

'Why not? I know I'm nothing special—'

She leaned sideways and kissed him on the cheek. 'Idiot! The reason I won't marry you is that I won't be a hanger-on at Nanselow.'

'Hanger-on! If you realized how much I need you . . .'

'Listen, Harold, I'll tell you what I'm going to do if I'm allowed to. I'm going to learn to do something worthwhile properly and it's not going to be medicine. I've really enjoyed working in the nursery and if I can get a job like that and do one of those courses at the Technical College in horticulture I would take it up as a career.'

'Have you talked to Nancy?'

'No, but I'm going to, and I shall have to discuss it with mother.'

'None of that would stop us getting married.'

'Perhaps not, but there's another reason against it. I'm not sure about having children. You know why.'

He looked at her, grave and anxious. 'I would leave that to you. If you decided not, I wouldn't mind.'

She smiled. 'Not now, you wouldn't, but a few months back you weren't bothered about Saunders's bad farming, the land-drains in ten-acre, or the rating assessment.' She put her hand on his thigh. 'In a couple of years, if not before, you'll be as concerned about the Succession with a capital S as your father ever was.'

He put his arm round her and kissed her eyes. 'You're laughing at me.'

'Am I?'

Saturday evening after supper Ethel was in her room entering up her journal. Care females had kept journals for generations and a shelf of fat exercise books written in Ethel's bold round hand recorded in stark simplicity the daily round of her life and that of the household through nearly seventy years, from Asquith and suffragettes to Margaret Thatcher and gay lib. Lacking any literary merit, they were scriptural in their authority on matters of what, when and where. She kept her door open while she wrote so that she missed as little as possible of what was going on.

There were footsteps on the stairs to the attics where John had his room.

'Is that you, John?'

'Yes, gran.' Unusually distant and non-committal.

'Come here, boy, I want to talk to you.'

John came and stood just inside the door, questioning, reluctant and a little sulky.

'Close the door and sit down, John.'

John had stored memories of his grandmother's room for he had always been her favourite; her room had provided the still centre of his childhood and it never changed; the blended odours of lavender water, moth-balls and a certain mustiness spanned the years.

John sat on the edge of a little tub-chair so that his knees were higher than his seat. The old lady stopped writing, closed her bureau and turned to him.

'Now, John, what's it all about? It's not a bit of use pretending you don't know what I'm talking about or that it's nothing to do with me or that it's because of you grieving for Laura. Naturally you're upset but that's not the whole story.'

John's craftsman's fingers were clasped round his knees. 'I'd rather not talk about it.'

'Good! That's honest. But you can't stop me asking questions. Of course you can walk out on me but you're far too well mannered for that.' She paused as though waiting for him to say something and when he didn't she shot out, 'It's to do with Laura, isn't it?'

John looked at her with troubled eyes but said nothing.

'She used to put you through it sometimes, didn't she? Laura was clever at needling people and she enjoyed it; especially with people like you, easily hurt yourself and not anxious to hurt others. That's you, isn't it, John? Not that you couldn't hit back if you wanted to—nobody doubts that.'

The old lady watched him, grave and calculating. 'Did she ever suggest to you that your father or your mother or both were responsible for her mother's death?'

She saw the startled look on the boy's face and thought that she had homed in the gold. 'Oh, don't look surprised. It wasn't only you. She didn't dare come straight out with that sort of talk to me but I could see the drift of her questions.

'Of course, you were very upset.'

John shook his head. 'Laura never suggested that to me.'

175

'She didn't?' Ethel was at sea. 'What was it then? There must have been something.'

'She hinted that father was also Alice's father.'

It was the old lady's turn to be surprised but she gave no sign. 'Yes, well, that's the kind of thing.'

'I didn't believe her.'

'No, but it was worrying, I can understand that. When we talk about *your* father and *your* mother and Laura's mother, we are talking about *my* son and *my* daughters-in-law—you see that, don't you? And, of course, Laura was *my* grandchild, as you are. What I am saying, John, is that we are in this together, we are not talking as strangers.'

John gave no sign that he had heard.

Ethel opened a drawer of her desk and took out a paper bag. She held it out to John. 'Going to have a peppermint? You've never refused one yet.'

John took one of the brown and yellow striped humbugs which Ethel still contrived to buy somewhere.

'I heard your mother say that you knew Laura was using the tower for her antics. Did you know that she would be up there the night she died?'

He moved the bulky sweet to a more convenient place in his mouth. 'I thought she might because I saw her going up there with a bag earlier in the day.'

'You didn't go up yourself that night to see what was going on?'

'No.' Emphatic and sullen.

'If you went out that night at all you might have seen her . . . I mean, you often go up to the badger set at night, don't you?'

'I didn't that night. In any case the set is on the edge of the plantation not East Wood.'

Ethel knew that it was essential to ask precisely the right questions; the boy would not lie to her but the best she could expect was laconic answers. She remembered that his attic room faced east and the little side door mostly used by the family was on that side of the house.

'Did you see someone from your bedroom window?'

It was distressing to watch the boy's face, flushed and tremulous, but Ethel was thoroughly Jesuitical concerning ends and means.

'Was it Laura?' She realized at once that it was a foolish question. He would scarcely have been upset at seeing Laura.

'Your mother?'

But she was too late. John had got up from his chair and he was at the door, he opened it and closed it quietly behind him.

Ethel sighed.

Chapter Ten

A KEATSIAN AUTUMN with plenty of mellow fruitfulness drifting into October; morning mists, yellow chestnuts, bronzed beeches and rich brown oaks. Nanselow seemed to have entered upon a period of calm, of domestic tranquillity. Celia and Nancy between them had made seventy pounds of jam, forty pounds of plum from their own trees and thirty of bramble jelly from blackberries picked by John. The freezer was stocked with blackcurrants and gooseberries, tomatoes, peppers and melons.

There was less acrimony in the kitchen; the three women seemed to have mellowed with the season. Celia had put on some weight despite the crisis over King's. Alice was working full-time at the nursery and attending classes at the Technical College. After a first dramatic outburst Celia had contented herself with mutterings about wasted talent which became less convinced and less convincing as the days passed.

'You could have done that with a couple of O-levels at sixteen!'

'I know, mother.'

Alice was learning about soft answers.

At any rate when Celia was introduced for the first time to the cuckoo-clock bedroom, Payne had been ungrudging in his admiration.

Isobel had been given her own column in a women's magazine, a welcome boost to her ego and her income.

Harold worked like Noah preparing for the flood, dividing his time between the estate office, the farms, and books on land, livestock, soil and crop management, and estate finance. He had negotiated a loan on the security of his expectations and repairs to the house were imminent.

John was back at school, still the same good-natured, willing, busy John; but a little more withdrawn, a little more solitary, and there were times when he seemed almost morose.

Henry worked at his gardening and his painting with an air of self-satisfied benevolence which was much in evidence when the whole family gathered in the kitchen for a catch-as-catch-can lunch. At such times he was apt to look over the assembled company with the air of one who says, 'I told you so.'

Part of Henry's contentment arose from his acquaintance with a lady in her mid-thirties whose invalid mother had recently died, and who saw it as her rôle to provide inspiration and consolation for male genius.

Only Ethel and Nancy remained unchanged.

On a Friday morning in early October when the three women were in the kitchen as usual a large yellow lorry drove into the yard and two men started to unload great quantities of steel tubular scaffolding. It was the first material evidence of their changed fortune and they were gratified.

Isobel looked out of the window. 'They're going to start on the roof.'

Celia said, 'Thank God for that! We can get rid of our chamber-pots.'

And Nancy added, 'They make good money in sales, especially if they have a floral pattern like ours.'

Miss Pearl came tripping over the cobbles and tapped on the door. She sorted her mail on the kitchen table. 'Three for Sir Henry, two for Lady Care, six for Miss Isobel, a new jig-saw for her ladyship . . . Mr Harold has had his at the office.'

Nancy said, 'I'll get Ethel's tray.' A pot of tea, one spoonful of Ceylon, one spoonful of China; two slices of bread-and-butter cut thin . . .

'Good morning, mamma.'

'Good morning, Nancy.'

Nothing had changed; the cat was on the bed, a half-completed

179

jig-saw covered much of the table in the window; Ethel was sitting up in bed.

'The men have come with the scaffolding to do the roof, mamma.'

'Ah! So we've made a start. On the way back.'

Nancy went over to the window and stood looking out. The course of the river was marked by white mist but the estuary was clear and sparkling in the sunshine.

Ethel bit into a piece of bread-and-butter. 'I'm quite good at jig-saws, Nancy.'

'Jig-saws? Yes, I know you are, mamma.' Nancy was puzzled, the old lady rarely said anything without a reason.

'Some people are, it requires a particular kind of nous—one has to recognize the similarity between the bit of the puzzle in one's hand and the space where it will fit. One needs a sense of shape, a sense of colour and, above all, a sense of pattern.'

Nancy said, vaguely, 'Yes, I suppose that's true.'

Ethel went on, 'Sometimes I think jig-saws would be more fun if they had a lot of extra pieces which didn't belong to the puzzle, which wouldn't fit anywhere. That way it would be more like life.'

'Like life?' Nancy asked softly.

'Yes. In real life it's difficult to know which pieces belong to a particular puzzle and which don't. But if one has a feeling for pattern they can often be sorted out.'

Nancy moved towards the door. 'Yes, I expect you are right.' She had her hand on the door knob. 'Well, I must be getting over to the nursery or they'll think I'm lost. Will you be coming over this morning?'

'Don't go, Nancy!' Ethel's tone was suddenly peremptory but as Nancy turned back from the door she was reverted to her former conversational manner. 'There's something I want to say to you. Perhaps it would be better left unsaid but it will remain between the two of us; I'm quite sure of that.'

The old lady moved her tray to the bed-side table as though symbolically clearing the decks.

'I never really believed that Laura killed herself.' Ethel allowed the words time to gather significance before adding, 'And accident, of course, was out of the question.'

Nancy stood rigid, her features set in a mould of bored acquiescence.

'Nobody seems to have thought of the possibility that Laura was not alone up there. Once that idea occurred to me bits began to fall into place.

'It was a summoning—that's what she called it, so I looked up what that meant in some of her books. You've never read such rigmarole, but I found what I wanted. It seems that the silly girl expected to summon up a spirit, some sort of demon who was supposed to answer her questions.' Ethel looked at Nancy with her compelling stare. 'Questions about how her mother died, I suppose.'

The old lady shifted her pillows and worked herself into a more comfortable position. 'When you and I think of a demon I suppose we think of the devil; horns, cloven hoofs, forked tail and trident; but, apparently, it's not like that. The demons when they appear are supposed to assume human form and often they take the form of someone well known to the summoner. One chap saw his naked mistress and another, himself, as if in a mirror . . . So if Laura really believed in all this nonsense it wouldn't have surprised her to see one of us.'

Ethel paused. It was so quiet that they could hear the clatter of steel tubes being unloaded in the yard behind the house. Nancy said, 'Well?'

'You were seen in the park that night, Nancy.'

Nancy's expression did not change in the slightest degree and Ethel went on, 'Apparently she was half-drugged by the smoke from the herbs she was burning and she would scarcely have known what was happening to her anyway. It probably wasn't difficult to manoeuvre her to the right gap but, just in case, you had a gun. Whatever happened, Laura mustn't come out of it alive.'

Ethel stopped speaking and Nancy waited, apparently to make

sure that she had finished, then Nancy said, in a voice that was almost normal, 'Well, I really must go now. Did you say that you would be coming over, or not?'

Ethel said, 'I shall be there.' And she added, after a moment, 'As usual.'